Clint heard the sound . . .

of the hammer on a gun, being cocked, and he reacted by reflex. There was only one reason for that sound to be heard behind a man's back, so he simply whirled, drew, and fired.

His bullet caught a stunned Manuel in the chest, punching right through and out the back. The Mexican's finger yanked convulsively on the trigger of the Colt, which fired into the ground. The man swayed and was dead before he fell to the ground.

The Gunsmith was holstering his gun, standing over the dead man, when more men suddenly arrived. . . .

Don't miss any of the lusty, hard-riding action
in the Charter Western series, THE GUNSMITH

And coming next month:
THE GUNSMITH #47: THE MINER'S SHOWDOWN

THE GUNSMITH

46
WILD BILL'S GHOST

J. R. ROBERTS

CHARTER BOOKS, NEW YORK

THE GUNSMITH #46: WILD BILL'S GHOST

A Charter Book / published by arrangement with
the author

PRINTING HISTORY
Charter edition / November 1985

ISBN: 0-441-30950-X

Charter Books are published by The Berkley Publishing Group,
200 Madison Avenue, New York, New York 10016.
PRINTED IN THE UNITED STATES OF AMERICA

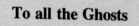

To all the Ghosts

ONE

No one knew how or where the rumor started, although many that had come to be regarded as legends had been started by the man himself. Still, this one couldn't have been started by him, could it? After all, the man was dead . . . wasn't he?

At least, that's what everyone who was in Deadwood at the time said, that Wild Bill Hickok had been shot from behind and killed by the coward, Jack McCall.

So how could he be alive years later, as the rumor now said?

Of all the men Clint Adams, the Gunsmith, had met during his adventurous and action-filled lifetime, none had commanded as much of his respect as James Butler Hickok, known to the public at large as Wild Bill Hickok. Not even his friends Bat Masterson and Wyatt Earp, who were rapidly becoming legends themselves, commanded greater respect than Hickok.

Hickok, by no means a perfect man or friend, was, nevertheless, there whenever the Gunsmith needed him and vice versa. When Hickok was marshal of Abilene in

'71 and needed another deputy, it was Clint Adams he sent for, and the Gunsmith had responded and pinned on a badge, though he had sworn never to do so again.

Hickok had been his friend, as no other man had been before or since, and when he was killed, Clint Adams was devastated and driven to the bottle. He had successfully crawled out of the bottle and had once again taken control of his life, but he had never quite recovered from the loss of the man he considered his closest friend.

Adams had been known many times to sit and talk about the legendary Wild Bill, as he was doing this night, in the Leadville saloon in Leadville, Kansas.

"When you get on this subject," Luke Short said, "there's no getting you off it."

Clint regarded Short over the rim of his beer mug and then lowered the glass to the table.

"You're right," he said. "I guess I've been known to bore people talking about Bill—"

"I didn't say I was bored," Short said, "just that you do go on. I don't think I've ever had a friend I could say I was that close to."

"You and Bill were friends, weren't you, Luke?"

"We knew each other," Short said, choosing his words carefully. Short had a long flowing mustache—as Hickok had for years—and he affected the gentlemanly attire of a professional gambler, which is what he was. He had been many things in his life—army scout, whiskey peddler, some said gunman—but he liked gambling the best, and it was the way he made his living. Among his friends were people like Wyatt Earp, Bat Masterson, and Hickok—all of whom were also friends of the Gunsmith's.

"We respected each other," Short went on, "and for all I know we may have even liked each other, although I don't take easily to many people. You and Bill, though, that was different. I don't think I've ever had a friendship quite like the one you had with him.''

"You will," Clint said, finishing his beer. "It's closing time, isn't it?"

Short checked his watch and said, "By Christ, it is at that."

Clint stood up and Short said, "Hey, you don't have to leave. Since I work here, I can keep it open as long as I like." Luke Short was a dealer in the saloon.

"Felicity is waiting for me at the hotel—or she should be by this time."

"If she should be, I'd say she is. That little lady has it bad for you, Clint."

"I like her, too."

"I'm not talking about liking you—"

"I know what you're talking about, Luke," Clint said. "Good night."

Clint Adams had been in Leadville for almost ten days now. The presence of Luke Short and, later, of Felicity Moran, were the reasons he had stayed that long.

Felicity was a willowy, auburn-haired girl he had met over lunch one day, while they were both sitting alone. Never a shy man, Clint approached her immediately, intrigued by the play of freckles across her face. He couldn't help but wonder how far they extended below her neck, and later that same evening he found out. Since then, they had met regularly.

Although she did not have a key to his room, she did have access—the clerk knew their arrangement—and she was indeed waiting there for him—naked and in his bed.

"Clint," she said as he walked in.

She sat up in bed, letting the sheet fall to her waist. Her breasts were small, peach-sized orbs, firm and covered

with freckles that were several shades lighter than her
dusky nipples. She complained that she didn't like her
freckles, but he had no complaints in that area.

"I've been waiting," she said. Then noticing the look
on his face as he turned up the lamp, she said, "What's
wrong?"

"Nothing."

"You've been brooding," she said, rising from the bed
to approach him. "I can tell."

Her hard little breasts almost glowed in the light, their
nipples dark brown, waiting for his fingers or his tongue to
excite them. She amazed him in that she refused him
nothing and took only what he offered. He'd seen that
before in saloon girls, but not very often in the kind of
woman who ran a general store, as Felicity did. Those
women often were more inhibited. Felicity was not like
them.

"Yes," he said.

"About what?" she asked.

"Old friends," he replied.

"What about present friends?" she asked, standing
directly in front of him. "Want to pay some attention to
us?"

"Yes," he said. He reached for her, scooped her up in
his arms, and kissed her, crushing her breasts against his
chest. Her tongue was alive in his mouth, avid, searching,
and she writhed against him, the friction bringing her
nipples erect.

He carried her to the bed, lowered her gently onto it,
and then undressed as she watched.

Felicity knew that tonight would be one of his gentle
nights. He'd caress her, kiss her, bring her body to life
with his hands and his mouth, and then she would do the
same for him.

He lowered himself onto the bed and began to kiss her—first her mouth, then her neck. He lingered on her breasts, biting the already distended nipples gently, sucking them until they were as hard as pebbles, and then he continued his journey down her small body, his lips at times seeming to barely touch her, until his head was nestled between her thighs, those glorious thighs. He reached beneath her to cup her taut buttocks and she tightened her thighs around his head as his tongue delved into her depths, tasting her sweetness, her tartness, and bringing her to a shattering climax.

Later they exchanged roles and her mouth traced a path down his lean, hard, and, in some places, scarred body until one hand encircled the base of his rigid penis, while the other gently, teasingly cupped his testicles. Her lips swooped down on him, taking the length of him inside, suckling him until he exploded, moaning, lifting his hips off the bed, filling her with his passion as she worked furiously over him until he was satisfied completely.

And later still he guided himself into her, and while she held on by locking her slim but powerful thighs around his waist, he drove both of them over the edge once again, this time together.

Resting in each other's arms they began to talk, and gradually he again fell into the subject of his old friend, Hickok.

She knew that, sooner or later, she'd get him to discuss what he'd been brooding about earlier.

"Luke told you, then?" she inquired.

"Told me what?"

"About the rumors," she added.

"What rumors?" he asked, sounding as puzzled as he actually was.

That was when Felicity began to think that perhaps she had made a mistake.

"Uh, Clint—"

"What rumors, Felicity?" he asked, propping himself up on an elbow.

"Maybe I shouldn't have said anything," she replied.

"It's too late now, honey."

"I guess you're right," she stated and told him about the rumor that Hickok had been seen in Mexico, on more than one occasion, very much alive!

TWO

Felicity was surprised when Clint rose, dressed, and left the hotel room to go and wake up Short in the middle of the night—which just showed that she had no idea how Clint felt about Bill Hickok's friendship. First of all, she did not realize that the friendship had not come very easily and, second, that it was not something that very many men could boast about.

Clint banged on the front door of the saloon until finally there was a lamp lit inside and someone began throwing back the bolts.

"What in blazes—" Luke Short started to demand, but as the door opened Clint put his hand on Short's chest, fingers splayed, and shoved. As the other man backpedaled to retain his balance, Clint entered and shut the door behind him.

"What's wrong?" a woman's voice called from upstairs. "Who is it, Luke?"

She came into view then, a pretty blonde with large breasts that were naked and pendulous. Clint couldn't help notice the rosy hue her skin had and that her nipples

7

were large and taut. She took one look at what was happening and her hands flew up to cover her breasts.

"Tell her to go back to the room," Clint said, glaring at Short.

"Go on back to the room, Holly," Short said. He had regained his balance and his feet were now firmly planted. He was wearing his pants, Clint saw, and the upper part of his longjohns. His hair was tousled.

"What the hell's gotten into you?" Short demanded.

"Why didn't you tell me about the rumor?"

"What rumor?"

"About Hickok being alive in Mexico."

"Oh, that!" Short said. "That's just a rumor, Clint, a story. Hickok's dead, you know that."

"I know I was told that," Clint said belligerently, "and so were all the newspapers, but I never saw a body, Short, so how do I know?"

"Jesus, Clint, you can't think—"

"Tell me about it," Clint said, cutting the other man off.

Luke Short stared warily at Clint Adams. Although he referred to the Gunsmith as his friend, the truth of the matter was that he really didn't know him all that well. He felt that Clint opened up to him about as much as he did to anyone, but did that make them particularly close friends? Not when you stacked it up against the bond of friendship that had existed between Adams and Hickok. You'd almost think the two men had been blood brothers or kin.

Many men regarded Luke Short as a gunman, but Short himself had no illusions about his chances going up against the Gunsmith. He decided he'd better tell the irate Gunsmith everything he knew.

"All I know is that I heard that he'd been seen several

times down in Mexico, near and around Mexico City.''

"Dressed how?''

"Red sash with two guns tucked into the front.''

"That's Hickok, all right,'' Clint replied.

"Clint, if somebody *wanted* people to think he was the second coming of Bill Hickok, wouldn't he dress just that way?''

"Maybe.''

"And if it is Hickok, then he's been laying low for years. Why is he all of a sudden strutting around in his red sash and Prince Albert waistcoat, shooting—''

This time Short stopped his question on his own accord, and Clint said, "Shooting? What's that about shooting?''

"Supposedly he'd been in a couple of gun battles, and people have sworn that they've never seen anyone draw a gun so fast.''

That was Hickok, too. Faster than God with a gun, maybe even faster than the Gunsmith. Neither man had ever had the need to find out who was faster.

Clint now had the need to find out if his friend was still alive, and if so, why he'd been playing dead all these years.

He turned on his heel and started for the door.

"Where are you going?'' Short called out.

"Mexico.''

"Clint, don't be a fool—''

"I'd be a fool if I didn't go,'' Clint said, turning to face Luke Short. "Even if it isn't Bill, I don't want someone toying with his memory, trying to cash in on his name and reputation. Luke, if there is someone in Mexico playing at being Bill Hickok, he's going to be one sorry hombre.''

"And if it is Hickok?''

"He's going to be sorry, too,'' Clint said, "for letting

me think he was dead all this time.''

"Clint.''

"What?'' Clint asked from the door.

"I kept it from you because I knew you'd do just this,''
Short said, crossing the floor. "Go running off half
cocked to Mexico looking for a dead man.''

"If you knew me at all, you would have told me as soon
as you heard,'' Clint said. Then he brought himself up
short and asked, "When did you hear?''

"I heard the first rumor before you came to town, and
others about a week ago.''

"Why didn't I hear?''

"I just . . . let it be known that it wouldn't be . . .
smart for anyone to tell you,'' Luke said hesitantly.

"Didn't you think I'd find out eventually?''

"I guess you would have . . .'' Short said, feeling a bit
helpless now. "Clint, I was just trying to help.''

"Go back to your ladyfriend, Short,'' Clint said.

"Are you—uh—coming back this way?''

"I'll be leaving my rig and team behind,'' Clint said.
"I'd appreciate it if you'd look after them.''

"Sure. Uh—Clint.''

"Yeah?''

"I'd be interested in what you find out,'' Luke stated.

Clint looked at Luke Short and allowed himself a small
smile.

"Sure, Luke,'' he said.

"Will you be coming back to Leadville?'' Felicity
Moran asked.

"To pick up my rig and team,'' Clint said, lifting his
hastily packed saddlebags and tossing them over his
shoulder.

"I understand," she said. She was sitting up in his bed with the sheet around her. "I've sorta been thinking of moving on, myself."

"Is that so?" he asked. He moved to the bed just long enough to kiss her fleetingly, then picked up his rifle, went to the door, opened it, and turned back to her again.

"Bye, Clint."

"We'll see each other again, Felicity."

"Sure," she said, "maybe even San Francisco, huh?" She talked a lot about going to San Francisco.

"Maybe."

Clint left, and Felicity Moran hoped that he would not find what he was looking for—but what was best for him to find.

The man with the red sash sat at a back table of the cantina, nursing a bottle of whiskey and toying with a deck of cards. He was a tall, broad-shouldered man with long, blond hair that hung past his shoulders, and a long, flowing, well-cared-for mustache. Tucked into his sash were twin .36 Navy Colts with the butts reversed.

His blue eyes steadily scanned the room, missing nothing, and when three men entered the room, he knew they were the ones he was waiting for, but he made no move to signal them. They, in turn, swept the room with their eyes, and when they spotted him, one of them spoke to the other two, and they approached the table.

Unconcerned, the man with the sash poured himself another drink.

The three of them were Mexicans—which was no surprise since they were in Mexico—and they all carried worn weapons and bandoleers crisscrossing their chests.

They were bandits, but they were bandits with ambition. Porfirio Díaz had not been in power long, yet already it was obvious that his rule would not be to the benefit of all the people.

One of these bandits wanted to be President of Mexico, and he was looking for men to help him achieve this exalted position. Already he had many mercenaries from both sides of the border working for him, but when he heard about *this* man—this gringo—now in Mexico, he hurried to this sleepy little Mexican town to meet with him, after first sending a message ahead. The reply to the message had been that the gringo spent much of his time in the cantina, and this was the situation that now existed as they approached him.

If they could get this man on their side—just this one man—he could turn the tide in their favor.

Such a man was the famous Wild Bill Hickok—a man whom the world thought was dead.

It was not until Clint Adams was crossing the Rio Grande River from Texas to Mexico that he realized what he was actually doing.

He halted Duke on the Mexican side and sat there a few moments, letting his thoughts settle down.

"Rumors," he said aloud, ostensibly to Duke, because talking to himself might have meant he was going crazy. He had never set much store in rumors before, so why now? Why had he allowed a few rumors to send him tearing across the country from Kansas to Mexico?

"To find a ghost," he said aloud to see if it sounded as ridiculous as when he thought it. "To find Wild Bill's ghost."

Now that he knew exactly what he was doing, he put his

heels to Duke and started up once again, heading for Mexico City. What the hell, it was the capital, and Hickok being Hickok—ghost or not—he'd eventually find his way there.

THREE

Clint's last stop in Texas had been Laredo, and his first stop in Mexico was a town called Nuevo Laredo. From that point—nearly Mexico's most northeastern point—it was at least 600 miles to Mexico City. If he pushed, he'd be in that city just inside two weeks.

He had pushed from Kansas to this point and felt that he and Duke needed some rest—especially Duke. The big black gelding had incredible stamina, but it wasn't boundless.

It was midday when they rode into Nuevo Laredo, and Clint decided that they would stay a day and a half before starting out again. Two nights' sleep in a real bed would have to carry him the rest of the way. For all he knew, during the weeks it had taken him to ride from Kansas to Mexico, the rumors could have stopped and the ghost disappeared.

He left Duke at the livery with special instructions to the liveryman for his care. He obtained directions to the hotel and went there to check in.

"Is there a telegraph office in town?" he asked the clerk after accepting his room key.

"Sí, señor," the middle-aged clerk said. He had slicked back, black hair and a thin mustache. "Go out thees door and turn right. If you walk three blocks, you will find it weeth no problem."

"Thank you."

"De nada, señor. Enjoy your stay and do not worry about the rebels."

"Rebels?"

"Sí, señor. Already many of the people are unhappy with Presidente Díaz. In Mexico, when people are unhappy, there are rebels."

"Where are these rebels?"

"Between here and the capital, *señor.* Are you traveling that way?"

"I am."

"Well then," the clerk said, changing his mind, "perhaps you should worry about the rebels."

"Thanks."

"But not while you are in town. Our law enforcement here is *excelente.*"

"Is it?"

"Oh, *sí, señor.* My cousin, he is the sheriff."

"How nice for you," Clint said. He picked up his saddlebags from the desk and his rifle from the floor and went to his room to drop them off. After that, he went in search of the telegraph office and found the clerk's directions flawless.

He sent a telegram to Labyrinth, Texas, addressed to Rick Hartman. Hartman had many contacts throughout Texas, New Mexico, and Mexico and was starting to spread out even farther. If the rumors were still alive, he'd be able to tell Clint for sure.

"I'm staying at the Hotel Laredo," he told the operator. "If I'm not in, leave the reply at the desk."

"*Sí, señor*, with my cousin."

"Cousin? Are you the sheriff here, too?"

"Oh, no, *señor*," the man replied, smiling broadly, "but my other cousin, he is the sheriff. Do you need to talk to him?"

He stared at the man's slicked hair and minuscule mustache and said, "I guess I do."

Unsure as to how large his reputation loomed in Mexico, he thought it best that he follow his custom of checking in with the sheriff whenever he hit a town.

The operator gave him directions and told him to enjoy his stay and not to worry about the rebels.

The sheriff's office was a wood-and-stone structure that, with its pitted and scarred façade, looked as if it'd had to withstand a few attempts to get in as well as to get out.

He knocked before entering because he knew that the Mexicans were very high on manners.

"May I help you, *señor*?" the man behind the desk asked. He was taller and slimmer than either the hotel clerk or the telegraph operator, but he had the same slicked back, black hair and thin mustache. On the desk in front of him was a half-eaten tortilla.

"Yes, sir," Clint said, approaching the desk as the lawman stood up. "I've just arrived in your town and would just like to—uh—check in with you."

"Check in?" the man asked, looking confused.

"Yes, introduce myself, let you know how long I'll be here, that kind of thing."

The man looked surprised.

"That is very unusual, *señor*," he said, studying Clint's face. "Are you perhaps wanted across the border by the law?"

"No," Clint said, holding back a grim smile at the

man's suspicion. "My name is Clint Adams, Sheriff, and I—"

"I see," the lawman said, and Clint knew he had recognized the name. "Now, I understand, Señor Gunsmith."

"Adams."

The sheriff matched glances with Clint and then executed a slight bow and said, "Your pardon, *señor*. I am Sheriff Sanchez. I appreciate your candor in coming to me. How long will you be staying in Nuevo Laredo, Señor . . . Adams."

"I'll be leaving in two days, Sheriff. I won't be here longer than that."

"Passing through?"

"Yes, I've come a long way, and I have a long way to go. I'd just like to get some rest for myself and my horse."

"Of course, of course. Where will you be going after you leave here?"

"I'm heading for Mexico City."

"Ah, the capital," the lawman said, nodding, prodding the remains of his lunch with a long forefinger. "Any particular reason?"

Clint thought a moment and then said, "I've never been there."

"Well, you should know about the rebels—"

"I've been told," Clint said, "by two of your cousins."

"Which two?" the man asked, frowning.

"How many do you have?"

"Many," he replied, laughing.

Clint told him which two, and the man nodded and said, yes, José and Ramon had been telling people—especially gringos—about the rebels.

"You have nothing to worry about while you are in

town, but between here and Mexico City—''

"Sheriff, I've interrupted your lunch," Clint said. "I apologize. Please, sit and finish it. I'm going to go and get something to eat and drink."

"The cantina down the street is very good," the sheriff said, seating himself once again. "My cousin Rosalita owns it and is the best cook in all of Mexico."

"Really?" Clint said, thinking about there being another cousin. Judging from what José and Ramon looked like, Clint was almost afraid to meet a female cousin. "I'll try it."

"You will enjoy it, *señor*. Good appetite!"

"You, too, Sheriff," Clint said and left.

Outside he paused and wondered if he hadn't made a mistake in announcing himself to the sheriff. The man had been suspicious when he mentioned Mexico City, and if there were rebels roaming about, what else was the lawman to think. Clint did, after all, have a reputation with a gun.

What he didn't need was for some Mexican lawman to think that he was in Mexico to try to overthrow the government.

FOUR

The cantina was a busy place, almost every table taken, and a chubby, dark-haired woman hurried from one to the other. Not only did she have dark hair on her head, but there were traces on her bare arms and upper lip, as well.

Cousin Rosalita.

As Clint entered, a small table opened up near a wall and he hurried to it and sat down. As he did so, the woman came over to clean the table and take his order.

"*Señor*?" she asked.

"Whatever your specialty is, I guess."

"Oh, *señor*," she said, boasting, "all of our food is special. Tortillas, tostados, enchiladas, chili—"

"Chili," he said, stopping her before she could go any further.

"Ah, you will love our chili, *señor*."

"And coffee?"

"Excellent coffee."

"And biscuits."

"Delicious."

"Your cousin sent me here. He said you had the best food in Mexico."

"My cousin?" she asked, frowning.

"The sheriff, Rosalita—" he said addressing her by name for the first time.

"Oh, *señor*, I am not Rosalita. She does the cooking. I an Conchita, the waitress. I will bring your food."

"Thank you, Conchita."

Watching her waddle to the kitchen, he was afraid to see what the real Rosalita looked like.

About ten minutes later Conchita came walking out from the back with another woman behind her, and if this were Rosalita, then Clint felt he had an apology to make to the woman.

"Here is your food, *señor*," Conchita said, attempting to put down the plates she was carrying. One started to slide to the floor and would have had it not been for the Gunsmith's reflexes. His hand shot out and caught it before it got away.

"I could not carry it all myself," Conchita said, "so I asked Rosalita to help."

Rosalita moved forward to place the last plate on the table, and she smiled at Clint, wiping her hands on her apron.

"This is Rosalita," Conchita said, also smiling. She actually had a very pretty smile along with the extra flesh on her face. Her breasts were like cannonballs beneath her blouse, and if she lost some weight—a lot of weight—she might have been a very pretty woman—like Rosalita.

"She is *my* cousin," Conchita went on, "but the sheriff is not my cousin."

Clint didn't even want to ask her how that worked. He preferred to look at Rosalita.

She was not as pretty as Conchita —Conchita could have been—yet they had a lot in common. Rosalita, too, had large breasts. The rest of her body, however, was not as heavy as Conchita's. Not that it was slim, however; she exuded a powerful, earthy kind of sensuality. And she knew it. Both women had dark hair and dark eyes and appeared to be in their early thirties.

As she looked at Clint, her gaze was openly admiring and bold, and he matched it.

"Hello, Rosalita."

"*Buenos días, señor*," Rosalita said. "It is an honor to have you in our cantina."

When she said that, he suddenly wondered if she didn't know who he was, but he discarded the thought.

"Enjoy your food," Rosalita said. He watched as she turned and walked back to the kitchen. Before she disappeared through the doorway, she turned and gave him a last look, and he felt as if a message had passed between them.

When he looked up at Conchita, he found her staring at him somewhat longingly, and he smiled self-consciously. It was odd, but Rosalita's frank appraisal had not unnerved him the way Conchita's was.

"Thank you, Conchita."

"*De nada, señor*. Please call me if you need anything else."

"I will."

After he was finished, he did call her and asked for another pot of coffee.

"Rosalita's coffee is good, no?"

"Her coffee, her chili, her biscuits, everything is good."

"I will tell her. She will be pleased."

He watched in amazement as Conchita almost pranced to the kitchen. A few moments later she and Rosalita came out, Conchita carrying the pot. Clint noticed that all of the men in the place watched Rosalita as she crossed the room.

"I appreciate your kind words, *señor*," Rosalita said, smiling.

"You deserve them, *señorita*," he said as Conchita bent over to place the coffee pot on the table, giving him a good view of the valley between her breasts. They appeared to be quite firm.

They left him to his second pot of coffee, and when he finished it, he paid his bill and left a little something extra for both women. As he was leaving, Conchita came rushing up to him.

"You are staying at the Hotel Laredo?" she asked, turning her puppy dog eyes on him.

"That's right. Why?"

She looked shy and said, "Rosalita wanted to know."

"Oh, I see."

He said good-bye and left the cantina, wondering if he was going to end up with some company that night—he hoped he would.

Clint went to the nearest saloon after eating, a small one with no gaming tables and two poker games going. He wasn't there to play poker, though, only to have a beer and relax. There was an empty table near the back so he took his beer there with him and tried to blend into the background—which, in a Mexican bar, is difficult for a gringo to do.

He received a few curious glances, but after about twenty minutes the other patrons seemed to accept him and stopped paying him any special attention.

He took the opportunity to think about Wild Bill Hickok. Bill had been thirty-nine when he was killed—just about the same age as the Gunsmith now—and that was some years ago. Surely he'd look the same now as he did then, wouldn't he? Clint couldn't imagine not recognizing Hickok if he were to see him again, but how realistic a possibility was that? It was true that he had never seen Bill's body, but there *were* friends of Bill's—Colorado Charlie Utter, for one—who had been present in Deadwood when the incident occurred.

No, more likely what he was looking for was someone trying to trade on Hickok's reputation, on the legend of Wild Bill Hickok, which would probably be enhanced for the imposter played the role of one supposedly dead. In this refurbished legend he would seem almost a god.

Wild Bill Hickok wasn't a god by any means but he did leave a legend behind, and the Gunsmith was going to make damned sure that legend was not sullied.

Sometime later Clint decided that he was doing much too much thinking about Hickok. He left the saloon and went to the hotel to get some sleep.

As a man who enjoyed women—and one women enjoyed—the Gunsmith had returned to many a hotel room in his life only to find it inhabited by a woman. More times than not, the woman was naked and in his bed.

On this night, he was hoping that he had read the look in Rosalita's eye right and would find her waiting for him in his bed.

He was disappointed.

As he entered his room and turned up the lamp he saw that it was empty. Briefly he entertained the thought of going back out to find some kind of female diversion, but he decided against it and began to undress for bed. He had his boots off and was naked to the waist when there was a knock at his door.

When he opened it, he was delighted to find Rosalita standing in the hall.

"Rosalita."

She smiled uncertainly and said, "I thought, *señor*, that this afternoon we were perhaps of one mind." She arched an eyebrow at him and asked, "Was I correct?"

She was wearing a blouse different from the one she had been wearing earlier that evening, and she had bathed. He could smell the freshness of her. Her mouth was lush and full, and a second ago she had been gnawing that lush lower lip. Now she smiled, revealing even, white teeth.

"You were correct," Clint said, matching the boldness of her gaze. She examined his chest as he examined hers; only she had the better view.

"Would you like to come in?"

She gave him a sly look then and asked, "Both of us?"

"Both of . . . who?"

She reached out with her right hand and pulled Conchita into view. Her cousin stood there next to her, looking at the floor shyly. She had also bathed and changed her clothes.

"Both of you?" he asked.

"We have agreed that you are much man, *señor*—"

"Clint."

"*Señor* Clint. Would you have us believe that you could not handle two women at the same time?"

"Well, no," Clint stammered. In point of fact, he did not have all that much experience with two women at once, having had the pleasure only two or three times. All those times, however, *both* women were either lovely or in some way lovely. Neither of them was ever the size of Conchita—and suddenly, Clint began to get curious. He looked at Conchita again. She had a pretty face, large firm breasts; she was just, unfortunately, overweight—though not grossly so.

"Come in," he said then. "Both of you."

FIVE

Rosalita pushed her cousin into the room ahead of her, and then she entered and closed the door firmly. Clint wondered if both women did this often.

"We do not do this often," Rosalita said, grasping the bottom of her blouse with both hands crossed. "Only when we see a man who appeals to both of us."

"Do you have similar tastes in men?"

Rosalita pulled her blouse up over her head and Clint watched with pleasure as her heavy, dusky-tipped breasts lifted and fell. They were well-rounded and firm and she bore them with pride, her chest pushed out unnecessarily.

"We both like men," she said, and Clint decided not to pursue the matter any further. He wasn't interested in their morals; he was only interested in a diversion for the night, and these two would certainly supply that.

Rosalita pushed her skirt down around her ankles and kicked it away. She hadn't bothered to put on any underclothes after her bath.

She was chunky, her large breasts well matched by large hips and meaty thighs—though he was willing to bet they were not as meaty as Conchita's.

Then he turned to look at Conchita, who was standing with her hands clasped in front of her, not looking at him.

"She is shy," Rosalita said.

"Rosalita—" he began, then stopped and changed direction. "Is there something I can call you two besides Rosalita and Conchita. They're kind of hard on a gringo's tongue."

Rosalita laughed and said, "You may call us Rosie and Connie."

"Well, that ought to be easier."

She laughed and Connie giggled. From the way her breasts moved beneath her blouse he could tell that she wasn't wearing anything underneath, either, and his curiosity about her was growing. He was actually becoming more interested in her than in Rosie.

"There's really no reason to be shy, Connie," he said, approaching her and placing his hand beneath her chin. He tilted her head up so he could look at her face and discovered that if a man looked past the obvious he'd find a very pretty woman.

Rosie said something to Connie in Spanish, and her huskier cousin smiled suddenly. Clint backed up and Connie reached for the end of her blouse and pulled it up and over her head.

Her breasts were very large, and there was almost no sag to them. Her nipples were the same dark brown as her cousin's.

Next, she dropped her skirt to the floor, but instead of kicking it away she simply stepped out of it. Her waist was not as pronounced as Rosie's, and her hips and thighs were heavy. He wondered, in spite of their heaviness, if they might not be firm, like her breasts. He wondered if this woman, who most men probably thought was fat, wasn't built and shaped just exactly as God had intended her to be.

He approached her then and gently reached for her breasts, cupping them in his hands. Her skin was baby smooth and he rubbed his fingertips against the undersides of her breasts while teasing her nipples with his thumbs. They swelled and tightened beneath his touch and her breathing began to come quicker. She reached out and began to run her right hand over his chest, playing with the hair and rubbing his nipples.

Her more direct cousin came up behind Clint and reached for his crotch, palming his erection through his pants, enjoying what she was feeling.

"Oooh, it's long and hard, Conchita," she told her cousin. "Weren't you getting ready for bed when we came, Clint?"

"I was," he said, still running his hands over Connie's breasts. He was marveling at their size, their firmness, at the fact that her nipples were almost as large as the tips of his thumbs.

"Are you too shy to finish undressing?"

He took his hands from Connie's breasts—reluctantly—and began to undo his belt. Connie's eyes dropped so she could watch. Rosie dropped her hand away so he could push the pants down over his hips and to the floor, after which he stepped out of them. He dropped his shorts next, keeping his eyes on Connie's face and saw her eyes widen at his erection.

From behind he could feel Rosie's cool hands slide over his buttocks and then her big breasts flattened themselves out against his chest.

"Kiss her," Rosie said from behind him, "kiss my cousin."

Clint reached for Connie and she came eagerly into his arms, mouth opening and breasts crushing up against his chest. Her mouth was hot, her tongue avid, and her arms went around him, her hands flat against his back. He could feel Rosie's mouth on his buttocks now, and then she was on the floor and her head was between his legs. Her tongue poked at his testicles and his erection seemed to swell even more as her wet tongue flicked along the length of it as well as it could with her cousin Connie in the way.

Connie moaned into his mouth as his hands slid behind her and cupped her buttocks, rubbing them and squeezing them.

"The bed," he heard Rosie's voice say, "put her on the bed."

Clint felt like a pawn between two queens. He pushed Connie back until she was up against the bed, and then he pushed her again and she went down on her back, just as easily as could be.

Clint was about to join her when he looked for Rosie and found her across the room, sitting on a chair with her knees up to her chest.

"I will watch," she said candidly.

"That's all?"

"For a while," she said. "I would like to watch for a while."

If someone had asked him at another time—any other time—if he could make love to one woman while another watched, he might have said no. Now, he found the prospect exciting. His heart was beating wildly, just about taking his breath away. He looked down at Connie and knew that if he entered her now he would explode almost immediately. He didn't want that to happen. He wanted to explore every inch of this big woman's body and, joining her on the bed, he proceeded to do so.

He kissed her neck tenderly, inhaling the fresh scent of her. Her hand strayed and made contact with his body wherever it could. His hand was flat on her belly and as he began to lick her breasts and bite her nipples he slid his hand down between her legs, finding her hot and wet. She moaned and strained as he aroused the very core of her and began to suck mightily on her nipple. In moments, she had an orgasm, her entire body drawing taut and then suddenly going limp.

He didn't stop there. He got onto his knees on the floor and pulled her to the edge of the bed so that her legs were hanging over the side. He ran his hands over her thighs, then down so that he could hold her legs by the calves and lift them up onto his shoulders. He was pleased to find that her thighs and calves were as firm as her breasts, and he decided there and then that this woman should not lose an ounce of weight because it was not necessary. She was fine the way she was.

He slid his hands between the mattress and her generous ass, cupped them that way, and began to flick his tongue over her, delving into her, tasting her, smelling her, *enjoying* her—and she was enjoying him. Her hips were twitching and she was bouncing in his hands. Her hands were gripping the edge of the bed as he licked the length of her. Connie, who had been quiet up to then except for an occasional moan of pleasure, began to babble aloud in Spanish now.

"She wants you to make love to her," Rosie said from behind, and it occurred to him fleetingly to ask her where she and her cousin had learned this technique. Probably from some gringo in her past.

He moved his head from her, his hands from beneath her, and he slid onto the bed with her. She pushed against the mattress, moving herself around on the bed to give him room, until her head was on the pillow. He got on next to her and she reached for him and pulled him down to her. He laid atop her on the cushion of her breasts and thighs, probed with the head of his cock until he found her wetness and slid into it, sheathing his rigid length in her heat.

"That's it," Rosie's voice said, close to his ear now instead of from across the room, "that's it, push it into her; she loves it, *we* love it, ummm—"

He was aware suddenly that Rosie was moaning along with her cousin, as if she could also feel what Connie was feeling.

Connie was crying out in Spanish again and Clint had no idea what she was saying. All he was aware of was her huge breasts beneath him, refusing to be totally flattened out by his weight, and the muscles inside of her pulling on him like a wet glove.

He was banging into her as hard as he could, his breath coming in rasps, as was hers. She clutched him to her, wrapping her heavy thighs around him. His cock felt huge to him, as if it were swelling and swelling, and yet it refused to explode. He pounded into her harder and harder and he could feel her body convulsing in a series of orgasms, but his own was seemingly trapped inside of him.

Suddenly, he was aware of Rosie's mouth moving over his buttocks, running along the crease between them, and then he felt her hands *part* his cheeks and probe . . . and he exploded!

He was filling Connie in incredible bursts while Rosie's tongue continued to probe from behind—a sensation he had never experienced before. As hard as it had been for him to achieve orgasm, it now seemed just as hard for him to stop. He kept filling the plump woman beneath him and she kept grabbing at him, scratching his back with her nails, jabbering in Spanish in his ear, and finally—mercifully—his ejaculation ceased and he and Connie began to gasp for breath.

Rosie had no intentions of allowing him to catch his breath, however, as she leaped on his back, her hard nipples scraping where Connie's nails had been. She kissed his neck and said urgently into his ear, "Me now, me, do it to me . . ."

The cousins proved to be more of a diversion than he had hoped for.

Later, during the night, he woke to find a weight on his chest. There was a similar weight across his hips and thighs. He opened his eyes and saw Rosie looking down at him from above her breasts, which were dangling in his face.

"Rosie—"

It stood to reason that the weight across his hips and thighs was Connie, and her hands were busily bringing his penis erect.

"Mmm," Rosie moaned, closing her eyes. She was sitting on his chest, rocking against his chest hair, and suddenly he felt Connie's weight lift and then come down on him, engulfing his penis in a tunnel as hot as the desert sun.

Connie was moaning, riding Clint up and down, and Rosie slid up and nestled the wet, fragrant lips of her sex onto his mouth. Clint, beyond the point of objecting, flicked his tongue out and she ground herself down on him so that he reached inside of her. She knew what she was doing, though, because she eased her weight off him after a few moments, so his tongue could reach up. He circled her stiff little nub with his tongue and she moaned again, cries mixing with those of her cousin, who was now sliding up and down his penis in mindless pursuit of the release her body sought. He began to move his hips in time with Connie's, sucking on Rosie until suddenly all three of them achieved orgasm scant seconds apart from each other—so closely together that it was almost like one mutual explosion.

When they woke him the next time, he came awake with a start, an objection on his lips that he couldn't possibly—but when he looked at them, he saw that they had both dressed.

"We must go," she said. "You need your rest, and we must open the cantina in time for breakfast, so we must also get some sleep."

Clint felt as if they had spent the entire night having sex in one way, shape, form or another.

"What time is it?"

"Four o'clock," Rosie said. "Still dark. You will come to the cantina for breakfast?"

"Uh—yes, sure."

"Sleep well."

First Rosie kissed him, her tongue darting fleetingly into his mouth; then Connie came to him, kissing him long and hard, her tongue lingering against his, and damned if, as they went out the door, they hadn't succeeded in bringing his penis to life again.

SIX

He woke four hours later and, surprisingly, felt curiously refreshed but for a weakness in his legs and loins. The four hours of physical rest, combined with the hours of mental rest—that is, hours when his mind had been concentrating only on the task at hand, satisfying the two cousins—seemed to have combined to refresh him.

He dressed, strapped on his gun, and thought fondly of the two women he had spent the night with, especially Conchita. He was pleasantly surprised to find her so sexually exciting and beautiful.

When he went downstairs to the hotel lobby, he noticed the clerk giving him a withering stare. Were the two women his cousins, too, and had he seen them leave the hotel? He decided not to worry about it.

Since he had promised them that he would go to the cantina for breakfast, he did just that and he was slightly uneasy at the attention they lavished on him. The Mexican men in the cantina were giving him looks that were less than friendly.

"Was everything all right, Clint?" Conchita asked.

"Everything was delicious, Connie," he said. "Tell Rosie for me."

"I will tell her," Conchita said.

As he stood up, she started to turn away, then turned back and put a hand on his arm.

"You are leaving town today?"

"Tomorrow, early."

She smiled and said nothing that her smile hadn't already said.

Clint left the cantina and decided to go to the livery to check on Duke's condition. When he got there, the liveryman was nowhere to be seen, so he entered, found Duke's stall, and checked the animal's condition.

"You're a wonder, Duke," he said, patting the gelding's massive neck. "Everything I've put you through and you're in perfect condition. Not even a stone bruise."

Duke swung his head around to look Clint in the eyes as if to say, what did you expect?

"I know, big fella," Clint said, moving around so he could rub the horse's nose, "but I had no right to expect it."

He took a few moments to be sure that Duke was being properly cared for, then walked out of the stall—and stopped short.

There was a group of men spread out in front of the door and he took a few seconds to count . . . eight. They were all armed.

"Can I do something for you?"

One man took a step forward, just far enough to single himself out as the spokesman. He was badly in need of a shave and a bath, but his eyes were clear. If these fellas had mayhem on their mind, it would have been better for the Gunsmith if they had been drunk—but at this time of the morning, they were all clear-eyed.

"We are loyal to our Presidente, Porfirio Díaz," the man stated.

"That's fine," Clint said, attempting to watch all eight men at once.

"Why are you here, gringo?" the man demanded.

"I'm just passing through," Clint replied, wondering if one or more of these men didn't fancy Rosie or Connie as their women and that's what had brought this on. Still, whether their intention was to kill him or just give him a beating, he didn't intend to make either one easy for them.

"No," the man said, "why are you in Mexico?"

"That's none of your business."

"If you are here to enlist as a mercenary with the rebel forces," the man said, pointing a finger at Clint, "then it is our business."

"Look," Clint said patiently, wanting to avoid trouble at almost any cost, "I'm not here to join anyone's forces. I'm here on private business. Now, if you'll let me pass we can call a halt to this nonsense—"

"Why should we believe you," the man said, bringing Clint up short after he'd taken one tentative step forward.

"Well, you asked me," Clint said, "you must have had it in mind to believe me or not. I'm telling you no, I'm not here as a mercenary."

He took another step and was standing right in front of the spokesman, who put a hand on his chest. Clint decided that this was a chance he couldn't pass up. He grabbed the man's wrist, twisted it painfully, and brought the man around with his arm bent up behind his back. One of the men went for his gun and Clint produced his and fired once, downing the man before he could reach his weapon.

"That's it," he shouted as the other men nervously considered going for their guns. "Tell your men to back out, friend, or I'll twist your arm off."

The man started to say something in Spanish, but Clint brought his arm up sharply, causing him to cry out in pain.

"In English, and tell them to pick up their friend and take him with them," he said, indicating the man he'd shot. The bullet had entered his left shoulder and the man was clutching at it, trying to stanch the flow of blood.

"All of you, take Nuñez with you and get out!"

The men all looked at one another, and then backed out, two of them pausing to pick Nuñez up and carry him out. Clint had the distinct feeling that they were relieved to be able to leave.

"You can let him go now," a voice said, and Sheriff Sanchez stepped into the livery.

"Maybe I should break his arm first, to discourage him from trying this again."

"I would not like that, *señor*," the sheriff said, stepping forward. He may not have liked it, but his gun was holstered. Clint holstered his.

"Don't tell me; let me guess," Clint said, releasing the man. "Another cousin?"

"No," the sheriff said, but before Clint could breathe a sigh of relief the lawman said, "This one's name is Sanchez. He is my brother."

Clint would have worried had not the words been spoken with distaste.

"Your brother?"

"He is a mercenary—" the other man began, but the sheriff backhanded him across the face, which Clint found somewhat surprising, since it was obvious that the sheriff was the younger of the two.

"Go with your friends and tell them not to bother this man again while he is in town."

Clint wondered why the sheriff made a point of finishing his sentence that way. Was he telling his brother that it was all right to try to kill him once he was out of town?

"I apologize for that," the lawman said, turning back to Clint.

"I'm sorry I had to shoot one of them, but he went for his gun."

"Knowing Nuñez," he said, "I'm sure he did. Shall we leave here?"

They left the livery, Clint feeling that perhaps the sheriff was escorting him to give him safe passage.

"I regret, Señor Adams, that it was I who mentioned to my brother that you were in town. I do not believe he told the others who you were, however, or they might not have followed him."

"Well, I hope there won't be any further trouble," Clint said sincerely. "Perhaps you would prefer if I left town today?"

"No, *señor*," the lawman said. "I would not ask you to leave town. You are welcome in Nuevo Laredo for as long as you stay."

"I appreciate that, Sheriff," Clint said as they reached the main street of town. "I'll be leaving in the morning, however."

"Very well," the lawman said. "I will try to keep my brother away from you until then. Please try to enjoy the remainder of your stay."

Again, as the sheriff left him there and started back to his office, Clint wondered why the man made a point of saying things such as he would keep his brother at bay until Clint was out of town.

Or maybe, he realized then, maybe it was his way of warning Clint Adams to be on his guard after leaving Nuevo Laredo.

The Gunsmith had never needed a warning to stay alert.

SEVEN

The remainder of the day went slowly, as Clint spent much of it at leisure. He sat on a chair in front of the hotel, relaxing but not letting his guard down. He went back to the cantina for lunch and had a delicious steak with even better service. In the afternoon he went by the telegraph office to see if a reply had arrived from Texas, and the clerk happily informed him that it had just come in.

"I was about to send someone to the hotel with it, *señor*."

"Thank you," he said, accepting the message from the clerk. He didn't read it until he was back in his room. It read:

> Can't add anything to what you know. Last heard rumor from Mexico City area. Can't be true, don't believe in ghosts. Luck on your search for the wild goose.
>
> Rick.

He couldn't blame Rick for that last remark. Rick Hartman was a sensible man who believed only in what he could see and touch.

Clint Adams had been like that, too. Maybe he was on this search to preserve that in himself. Find the imposter, see him, and touch him up good!

He folded the telegram, put it in his pocket, then took precautions before laying back on the bed. Nobody would be able to force the door or the window without setting off a racket. He'd used a pitcher and basin to fix that up.

He took a nap, just in case Rosie and Connie came back that night. If they did, he'd need all the rest he could get.

He had dinner at the cantina, spent some time in the saloon, and then went back to his room. This time the two women *were* waiting for him inside, naked and in his bed.

"How did you get in?" he asked, as he undressed to join them.

"The desk clerk," Rosie said, and Connie finished, "is our cousin."

"I shouldn't have had to ask," he said, approaching the bed. Clint wondered if he'd have the strength by morning to leave the room, let alone town.

In the morning Clint slid from between the warm, firm-yet-soft female bodies and began to dress quietly, watching them. They had proved over the past two nights that they were not shy in the least when it came to him. The two women were insatiable and inventive, and he wondered how many other strangers in town they had showed this much hospitality to in the past. He would like to think he was one of few, but he had his doubts. Their appetites would not go unsatisfied for very long. He appreciated them and that they had made Nuevo Laredo a place he would remember for a long time to come.

There were a lot of places in his past he remembered,

some for the right reasons and some for the wrong ones. This one he'd remember for the right ones: Rosalita and Conchita.

He slipped from the room without waking them, checked out, and retrieved Duke from the livery stable without running into any of the sheriff's relatives— specifically his brother, or his brother's unfriendly friends.

He settled up with the liveryman and turned Duke in a southerly direction. The liveryman told Clint that if he rode a few hours to the east, he could ride along the beach or bathe in the waters of the Gulf of Mexico.

It was something Clint might have liked to see, but he had a ghost to find.

He headed for Mexico City, wondering what he would encounter between here and there.

EIGHT

Clint was two days out of Nuevo Laredo when he realized he was being followed.

He felt it on the back of his neck. He had been feeling it for some time, but this time when he turned around he saw just the hint of dust behind him.

"We got company on our tail, Duke," he said, patting the big fella's neck. "Wonder if they're out of Nuevo Laredo, just going in the same direction?"

Duke shook his massive head, and Clint said, "Yeah, I know. Neither one of us believes in coincidence."

Clint looked behind him again, then looked east and said, "Maybe we should go and have a look, huh, Duke? What do you think?"

Duke's head bobbed and the Gunsmith chose to believe that the big head was nodding in agreement.

"That's one thing about you, Duke," he said, rubbing the horse's neck affectionately, "I never get an argument out of you."

He jerked Duke's reins to the left and then let him have his head to go as slow or fast as he preferred. The big gelding, constantly full of run, chose to do just that, and Clint felt that his speed was more than a fair exchange for whatever dust he was kicking up.

47

Clint smelled the water before they reached the beach, and he enjoyed the fresh salt smell of it. The closest he'd ever been to an ocean was San Francisco, and that had been from the Barbary Coast docks. This was something quite different.

As they reached the sandy beach, Duke balked at the soft, deep sand, and Clint allowed the horse to acclimate himself slowly until he finally agreed to walk on the sand.

"Won't hurt you at all, Duke."

He directed Duke to the water's edge, where the sand was wet and not as soft because of it, and they rode along there for a while. Watching the waves roll gently to the beach was a kind of lazy experience and Clint knew that if he weren't careful he could be lulled almost to sleep by it—asleep and dead, if he weren't *extra* careful.

The sun was riding high in a cloudless sky, reflecting off the water, and Clint thought it would be nice to be able to take a swim. Duke had sniffed at the water a couple times and had come to the conclusion that it was not fit to drink. Clint dismounted, poured some water into his hat, and held it for Duke to drain. After that he took a swig, replaced the canteen, and was in the act of mounting when he saw the riders.

There were four of them and they were behind him. They had just ridden onto the beach at the same point he had, and Clint frowned, trying to recognize them. He assumed they were Mexican from their large sombreros, although that certainly wasn't enough to support such an assumption.

He mounted and gave Duke a little kick in the ribs. They couldn't have been the riders who had been raising the dust behind him. There hadn't been enough time for them to catch up to him.

An uncomfortable thought had occurred to him, then.

The sheriff's brother had had seven men with him in the livery. What if four of them started out before Clint, and the other four after him, deliberately kicking up a great deal of dust so they would be spotted?

He'd been herded to the beach, he realized uncomfortably, where there was no cover for him.

He looked behind him and the riders were moving along slowly, matching his pace. He increased Duke's speed and, looking back, saw that the riders had increased theirs as well.

"All right, Duke," he said, "let's see how all of us handle the sand."

He gave Duke a big kick with his heels and the black horse's muscles bunched and he took off. Clint didn't bother looking back because he knew what he'd see. A few seconds later he heard the shots and he knew they were in pursuit.

He risked a look back at that point and saw that he and Duke were gradually increasing the distance between themselves and the four riders, all of whom were firing now. He was actually confident that he'd be able to lose them and was in no need of the help that suddenly materialized from his right.

Three riders came racing onto the beach, guns drawn, and began firing at his pursuers. Apparently the four pursuers did not like the fact that the odds had evened up, and they veered off, turning their horses, and fled.

Clint reined Duke in and watched two of his rescuers continue the chase while a third man stopped, turned, and rode back toward him.

The man approaching him was clearly Mexican, and as he reached Clint he holstered his weapon and smiled, revealing a prominent gold tooth.

"*Señor*," he said, "*buenas días*."

"Hello."

The man turned to look back and his first words were lost before he turned back, saying ". . . be bothering you for some time. Those kind, they are cowards. They will pursue a lone man, but will not face as many as they are."

"I appreciate your help," Clint said, although he didn't feel he'd needed it. "I must tell you, though, that they have four others they will soon join, and then they may come back."

"Fear not," the man said confidently, but did not elaborate about why the Gunsmith should believe him.

"Where did you come from?"

"Come," the man said, "I will show you. The *padrino* will want you to join him for lunch—if it is your pleasure."

"By all means," Clint said, "lead the way."

NINE

The house was set back from the beach so that it hadn't actually been built on the sand, yet the first step out the front door sat right on the beach.

"Impressive," Clint said.

The house was built of adobe and lumber—adobe walls and wooden ceilings. It was fairly large with a small barn behind it that didn't appear large enough to hold more than five or six animals. Still, the intention of the owner was clearly not to raise any kind of stock—unless it was fish or sand worms.

"Who lives here?" Clint asked as they pulled their horses to a stop alongside the house rather than in front, where they'd have been standing hock deep in sand.

"You will see, *señor*," the man said, dismounting.

Clint dismounted, growing more and more curious about the man who had built and now lived in this house by the beach.

"Come," the man said, waving for Clint to precede him to the front door.

When they reached the door, Clint found it constructed of thick oak, and as his guide pounded on it, he realized that this house was constructed very much like a fortress.

When the door was finally opened, Clint was surprised to find a young, Mexican girl wearing a plain skirt and peasant blouse standing there. She had long dark hair and dark skin and couldn't have been more than seventeen.

"Carlotta," the man said. "A man to see your father."

"An American?" she asked, in flawless English.

"*Sí.*"

"Father will be pleased," she said, but the appraisal she was giving Clint clearly stated that she was pleased as well. "Please come in. My father is in his office."

Office, Clint thought. What kind of a business could a man run from this location?

She closed the door behind them and Clint was surprised to feel how cool the house was inside. The adobe must have been very thick.

"This way, please," she said, walking ahead of them. Her skirt did not cover her calves, which were slim but well-muscled. Her feet were bare, and they were a little larger than one might have expected for a girl her size— five feet five, or thereabouts.

She led them down a cool hall to another oak door—this one not as thick—on which she knocked. A man's voice called for them to come in, and the girl opened the door.

"Father," she said, standing to one side, "an American."

"An American?" the man asked. As Clint entered, he saw a very tall, slender man behind a desk. He had been seated, but now he stood and hurried around the desk.

"My dear fellow," he said, as if Clint were an old friend he hadn't seen in years, "what a pleasant surprise."

Clint was a bit at a loss by the greeting and simply shook hands with the man wordlessly.

"I'm sorry," the man said, suddenly, "you must think me mad to greet you so, like a lost son, but I have so few opportunities to talk with Americans. Please, sit and we will introduce ourselves."

He directed Clint to a straight-backed wooden chair and circled his desk to sit once again in his own chair, which was made of red leather with gold studs.

"Carlotta, some brandy, please," the man said to his daughter, and then he looked at Clint and said, "That's all right, isn't it?"

"Fine."

"*Padrino*—" the Mexican said, stepping forward.

"Yes, Paco?"

Briefly, Paco explained to the man how he had come across Clint being pursued by four men on the beach, and the *padrino* listened intently until the man finished his story.

"Well, how fortunate for you that my men were out riding," he said to Clint, then. "Paco, please, see to our guest's horse."

"It would be an honor," the Mexican said, and then turned to Clint and added, "Such a magnificent animal."

At that point Carlotta stepped in front of Clint and handed him a glass of brandy, and it struck him how the same word might apply to her. Her face was startlingly lovely, her eyes large and dark, her eyebrows deep black, and her mouth wide, with a full, lush lower lip.

"Thank you," he said, accepting the glass.

Paco left the room and after Carlotta handed her father a glass of brandy the man dismissed her, saying, "That will be all, Carlotta. Tell Tía Maria that we will have a guest for lunch." He looked at Clint and said, "*Señor?*" asking for confirmation.

"My pleasure."

"Ah, good. Go, Carlotta, go."

"Yes, Papa."

She gave Clint a sidelong glance and then hurried from the room.

"All right, my friend," the man said, "my name is Jonathan Braxton . . . and you are?"

"Clint Adams."

"Of course," the man said, and Clint couldn't tell whether or not the man recognized the name or not. He *felt* that he had, but he vowed never to play poker with this tall, slender man who appeared to be in his early fifties.

"Were these men who were chasing you your enemies or . . ."

"I don't know who they were, Mr. Braxton."

"Please, call me Jonathan."

"Jonathan."

"And I will call you Clint."

"That's fine."

"Good."

"I have a suspicion that they might be part of a group I had some trouble with in Nuevo Laredo, but I can't be sure. I told Paco that if they were the same men, they would return in force."

"I can put together a force of four or forty at a moment's notice, Clint, so don't worry about endangering my family or myself. We are quite safe inside my—ah—house."

"It's quite impressive," Clint said, honestly. "Almost like a small fort."

"Yes, I built it myself. The house I always wanted—and the home."

"You said your family. You have others beside your daughter?"

"Actually, no," Jonathan said. "I had a wife, but she died . . . some time ago. It is only myself, Carlotta, and Tía Maria who cooks and cleans."

"And Paco?"

"He doesn't live here."

"Oh, I thought perhaps he and Carlotta—"

"No, no, no," Jonathan said, shaking his head. "I have much better in mind for Carlotta now that she is a young woman. She's eighteen, you know, nearly nineteen."

"I would have guessed younger."

"When she dresses for dinner, you will see," Jonathan said, and it was the first indication that he was expected to stay for dinner as well as lunch.

"You're not Mexican," Clint observed.

"Dear me, no," he said. "Actually, I'm part English and part German. I came here to Mexico years ago, with Maximilian . . ." The man trailed off, perhaps because he had caught himself saying too much to a stranger.

"What brings you to Mexico, Clint?"

"I'm looking for a friend."

"May I ask who?"

"May I ask what you did for Maximilian?"

Jonathan Braxton smiled first, and then laughed heartily and said, "I like you, Clint. Yes, we can talk about these things over lunch and then, I hope, over dinner?"

"Lunch, anyway."

"Ah, and perhaps dinner? We can talk about that later. Come, lunch should be ready."

As if on cue, there was a knock on the door and then Carlotta stuck her head in to say that lunch was served.

To Clint, lunch was an elaborate affair, but apparently

it was what they did everyday. The table was covered with Mexican food, and Braxton told Clint—in an obvious attempt to get him to stay for dinner—that dinner was always a mixture of Mexican and Texan cooking— something Braxton took great pride in dubbing Mex-Tex.

At the table Carlotta sat quietly while the two men talked, but her presence was definitely felt by the Gunsmith, even though she never said a word. Her eyes were on him. This he knew even without the glances he threw her way from time to time.

"What I did for Maximilian," Braxton said during lunch, going back to the subject himself, without prompting. "I told Maximilian what weapons to use. He made me an officer—a major—but I was really simply in charge of his armory."

"You're a weapons expert, then?"

"I suppose you could say that," Braxton said. "I respect weapons, most specifically guns." When he said that, Clint noticed that the man was watching him intently.

"Why guns?"

"Their potential is unlimited," Braxton said, "don't you think? Their power, their range, their very size, it is all so without limit that it's intensely exciting."

Clint could think of many things he found more exciting than guns—and one of them was seated to his left, with her big eyes on him.

Tía Maria—a portly, friendly looking Mexican woman who was Braxton's sister-in-law—came in and cleared the table, and Braxton told Carlotta to go and get the brandy decanter from his office.

"We have much to talk about," Braxton said to Clint after Carlotta had left the room.

"Like what?"

"Wait," Braxton said. "I will send Tía Maria and Carlotta away and we can discuss business."

"What kind of business would we have to discuss?"

"What kind of business," Braxton asked, "would one discuss with the Gunsmith?"

TEN

Carlotta brought the decanter and two crystal glasses and her father told her to take Tía Maria and find something to do in another part of the house.

"Yes, Papa."

"She's very sweet," Clint said after the girl had left the room.

Braxton laughed and said, "Don't let her fool you. She's being on her best behavior because we have a guest."

"I see."

Braxton poured the brandy and surprised Clint by leaving his place at the head of the table and coming to hand him the glass and sit near him, where Carlotta had been sitting during dinner.

"Clint, let me be honest."

"Don't let me stop you."

"I am still in the weapons business and I could use a partner."

"Not interested."

"You have not yet heard my offer," Braxton said. "Please, I am your host."

"I'm sorry," Clint said. "Go ahead."

Braxton nodded happily and launched into his pitch.

"There is a revolution brewing here in Mexico, and the rebels are going to need weapons, lots of them. That is where you and I come in. Most of these weapons we will buy cheap and sell high, but some of them we will build, you and I." Braxton rolled his eyes and said, "The guns we could build, Clint, you and I."

Braxton's eyes went to Clint's hip and they glittered and shone.

"May I?"

Clint, because the man had such a love and respect for guns, took out his modified Colt and handed it to Jonathan Braxton.

"Marvelous craftsmanship," the man said, examining it. "It is double-action, is it not?"

"Yes."

"You modified it yourself?"

"Yes."

"Marvelous," the man said, handing it back. "Do you know how a revolution could turn if one side were armed with double-action weapons?"

"Which side?"

Braxton shrugged and said, "Whichever can best afford our exorbitant prices."

"I'm not interested, Jonathan," Clint said, placing his empty glass on the table.

"Not now," Jonathan said, looking confident. "Do me the honor of staying for dinner and overnight. Think about my offer. We could be rich men."

"You seem to have all that you want right here, Jonathan."

Braxton sat back and said, "I am comfortable, but money would allow me the luxury of knowing that I could leave here if I wanted to. In other words, if I am here because I want to be it would be much more pleasurable than if I were stuck here—without money," he said, spreading his hands helplessly. "I am stuck here. Do you see?"

"I see."

"Then you will stay?" Braxton asked. "I will have my men scout for your enemies and assure you of safe passage in the morning—should you decide to leave."

Clint was thinking when the man asked, "Do you play chess?"

"I haven't in years," Clint said. He did not even remember the last time he had thought of the game, but he did remember hours of pleasure he'd derived from it in the past.

"Come," Braxton said, standing up, "you never forget how to play chess. It is all strategy—like war."

Clint stood up and Braxton motioned for him to bring his glass as the man lifted his glass and the decanter and led the way to the sitting room.

Braxton won the first game easily, and the next two not so easily.

"You are a good tactician," he told Clint as they played the fourth game, "but you must learn to strike directly, forcefully."

"Like this?" Clint asked. He moved his knight, successfully forking Braxton's queen and queen's rook.

"Yes," Braxton said with a frown, "like that."

They went on with the game and it went right down to endgame, Clint winning by attrition.

"Another?" Braxton asked.

"I don't think so," Clint said. He looked at the brandy decanter and saw that it was empty—and it was the second such decanter of the day. "I'm feeling very tired. My horse—"

"Is well taken care of, I assure you. My barn is small, but every effort is being made to accommodate him comfortably."

"Good," Clint said, rising, "then I'll say good night, Jonathan."

"One thing before you go."

"Yes."

"I've told you about Maximilian," Braxton said. "What about your friend? Who are you looking for with such determination that you would turn down the opportunity to be a rich man?"

Clint rubbed his jaw and then sat back down opposite Braxton.

"I'm tracking down rumors, Jonathan," he explained.

"What rumors?"

"Have you heard stories about . . . Wild Bill Hickok being seen in Mexico?"

"Hickok," Braxton said. "There was a marksman, eh?"

Clint had rarely heard Bill called that before, but he readily agreed.

"They say he was the fastest," Braxton asked. "Was that true?"

"I never saw anyone faster."

"Including yourself?"

"We never bothered to find out who was faster," Clint said.

"No, of course not, you were friends . . . and now you are seeking your friend."

"My friend," Clint said, "a ghost, or an imposter. Have you heard the rumors?"

"I have," he said, "and I'm sure the rebels have."

"The rebels?"

Braxton nodded.

"If a man like Hickok were alive and in Mexico, the rebels would try to recruit him . . . just as they will try to recruit you once they hear of your presence. Mark my words."

Clint explained briefly the encounter he'd had with the men in Nuevo Laredo.

"Porfirio Díaz has some loyal followers, but for the most part the people are beginning to see that he is not a leader who is for the people."

"What do you feel? Díaz ousted Juárez who overthrew Maximilian."

"Maximilian and I had parted company long before that," Braxton said, "but about the rumors—yes, I've heard them. I've heard he was seen around Mexico City and in Mexico City."

"Where around Mexico City?" Clint asked. "Can you give me the name of a town?"

Braxton thought for a while and Clint thought the man was going to try to trade his information, but quickly discovered that he had misjudged Braxton.

"I heard some talk about a small town called Acambaro," Braxton said. "It is about twenty, twenty-five miles from the capital."

"He was there?"

"So I have heard."

"When? How long ago?"

Braxton pursed his lips and let some breath out from between them slowly. Then he said, "A week, maybe more. By now he could be in the city or many miles away. He could be back in the United States."

"If he is," Clint said, "I'll track him there, too."

"Not until you get some sleep though, eh?" Braxton

said. "I'll have Carlotta show you to your room."

"That won't be nec—"

"She would insist," Braxton said, standing up. "In the morning we will talk again, eh?" His host extended his hand.

"In the morning," Clint said, taking the man's hand and shaking it, "but I won't change my mind."

"We will see," Braxton said and went to find Carlotta.

ELEVEN

Carlotta came to the sitting room while Clint was studying the craftsmanship of Braxton's ivory, oriental chess set.

"Beautiful, isn't it?"

He looked up as she entered the room and said, "Yes, it is."

"Papa made them," she said, coming right up next to him so that her hip was against his thigh and he could smell the fresh fragrance of her hair.

"Really?" Clint asked, looking more closely at them now.

"Has he offered to show you his workshop yet?"

"No," he said, looking at her, "no, he hasn't."

"He'll do that in the morning," she said, "over breakfast, to try to get you to stay a little longer."

"I see," he said, smiling and putting a chess piece down.

"Come on, I'll show you to your room."

As he followed her down a hall to a stairway, he said, "You speak English without any trace of an accent."

"Papa taught me English," she said. "Mama was

Mexican, so Spanish was easy. It was what I heard the most.''

Upstairs she led him down a hall to another oak door—Braxton had apparently used oak for all the doors to make sure they all did what doors are supposed to do—and opened it for him.

''This is your room. Paco brought your things in from the barn.''

''That was nice of him.''

They stood there in the doorway for an awkward moment and then she said, ''The bed is very comfortable.''

''Well, good,'' he said. ''Your father seems to specialize in either making or getting the best.''

''Maybe that's why he wants you to be his partner.''

''That's flattering,'' he said. ''Thank you, Carlotta. Good night.''

He stepped into the room and when he tried to shut the door he couldn't. Carlotta was in the way.

''Carlotta—'' he began.

She slid past him into the room, shut the door, and then turned to face him. Looking past her, he saw that the bedspread was very frilly and feminine, as were some of the room's other contents.

''Wait a minute—'' he started.

''This is my room, too,'' she said.

''This is your room.''

''Right.''

''I can't—''

''Papa told me to make you comfortable,'' she said, eyeing him boldly. She grasped the bottom of her peasant blouse—reminding him of Rosie and Connie, but only in that way—and pulled it up over her head. Her breasts, small, firm, tipped with brown nipples, made him twitch with anticipation.

"Carlotta, I couldn't," he said, "not in your father's house."

She dropped her blouse, moved toward him, and put her arms around his neck. Her breasts pressed against his chest like warm little puppies looking for a home.

"It's my house, too," she said. She pulled his head down and pressed her warm lips to his. He resisted as long as he could—about three seconds—and then put his arms around her and pushed his tongue past her lips into the hot cavern of her mouth.

She moaned into his mouth and slid her breasts back and forth across his chest, pressing her crotch tightly against him as well. He slid his hands into the waist of her skirt intending to ease it down over her slim hips but it came off before he even pushed it. He stroked her warmly and reached for her buttocks. The cheeks were smooth and soft in his hands, very different from those of the two women in Nuevo Laredo—but just as arousing, if not more so.

Carlotta was young and fresh. She smelled like new flowers; she had a youthful eagerness; her tongue avidly invaded his mouth, inspecting every inch of it, and yet she wasn't without experience. Her hands were between their tightly pressed bodies, kneading him through his pants. He slid one finger along the crease between her buttocks, and she started desperately to undo the belt of his pants, but his gunbelt was in the way.

"Please," she said, sliding her mouth just far enough away from his to form the words, "please, Clint."

"Easy," he told her, taking her by the shoulders and holding her at arm's length. "Your father mustn't know about this."

She smiled slyly and asked, "What makes you think he doesn't already know?"

"Carlotta—"

"Come," she said, backing away from him, "my bed is your bed."

She continued to back up until she was beside the bed, and then she sat on it, waiting for him. Shaking his head, he undid his gunbelt, hung it on the back of a chair, and moved to the center of the room to undress.

Carlotta watched him with obvious delight, licking her lush underlip as he slid his underclothes off, revealing his penis, erect and pulsing.

"Oh yes," she whispered as he approached the bed. "When I saw you, I felt something in here," she said, touching her stomach. "Do you know the feeling?"

"I know it," he said, reaching for her breasts. He cupped them, squeezed them, thumbed the nipples as she closed her eyes and leaned into him.

"I feel it again, even more," she said breathlessly. "What is it?"

Perhaps he'd been wrong in assuming that she *wasn't* innocent. Maybe she was just acting on instinct.

"Desire, Carlotta," he said, kneeling on the bed and pushing her down onto her back, "or you could call it . . . lust."

"Do you feel it, too?"

"Yes," he said, leaning over to run his tongue over her breasts, "I feel it."

"Oh," she moaned as he bit her left nipple.

"Shh," he cautioned her, "not so loud."

"I'll . . . try," she said hesitatingly.

Her skin was incredibly smooth, almost like warm marble, and as he mouthed her breasts he slid his hand down between her legs, finding her wet and waiting.

Suddenly, he couldn't wait. Everything else would have to come later in the night; right now he wanted nothing more than to plunge himself into her young body.

He positioned himself above her, prodded her opening with the head of his cock, and then eased into her. He was surprised that she was a virgin. There was the resistance and she was biting her lips, waiting.

"You don't mind, do you?" she asked, looking at him as she were afraid that he would withdraw.

"I don't mind, no," he told her, "but your father—"

"My father thinks I'm experienced," she said. "With all the men that ride through here, he expects it—but this is the first time he's getting what he expected—with you. I never expected. I never wanted any of those other men, but I wanted you as soon as I saw you, Clint. Does it happen like that?"

"Very often," he told her, kissing her. Her underlip was firm and full and he bit it and sucked it, kissed her avidly. He circled her tongue with his, kept her attention on what his mouth was doing as he eased more fully into her. He pressed the swollen head against her and suddenly her eyes widened.

"Don't worry," he said gently, kissing her. He prodded her again, then withdrew, gradually weakening her grasp on virginity, stretching it almost to the point of breaking.

He ran his mouth over the side of her neck on to her shoulder, bit her, licked her, distracted her—and then drove himself completely into her, imagining that he could hear her virginity exploding under his manly pressure.

He was deep inside of her then and she was crying out against his shoulder, holding him tightly, bathing his shaft in glorious heat as he took her in easy but long strokes. She was barely able to contain her pleasure each time he drove into her, and then suddenly she was all frenzied

movement beneath him as she experienced her first orgasm.

"Oh God . . ." she said against his shoulder, using it
to muffle her cries so no one would hear. "I can't . . .
believe it . . ."

His own release was rushing up through him now and
he said, "Hold on!" urgently, cupping her buttocks,
drawing her tightly to him. Then he filled her virgin
cavern with his milky seed and she bit his shoulder hard,
drawing blood.

And that only seemed to feed her excitement more.

"Does it hurt?" she asked him later.

He looked down at his shoulder, which was still oozing
a bit of blood, and said, "Of course, it hurts, woman. You
took a piece out of me."

"Oooh," she said, leaning over and licking the blood
away, "I'm sorry, but it was delicious." To emphasize
that, she took another lick. It was as if she really enjoyed
the taste of his blood.

He wondered what kind of a tiger he had awakened.

"Don't be sorry," he said, caressing her face. "You
had no control."

"I didn't! It was incredible," she said, her eyes wide,
incredulous. "Is it like that every time?"

"Almost," he said, "and sometimes it's even better."

"It couldn't be," she said. "Oh, it just couldn't feel
any better."

"There are many different ways to feel pleasure, Carlotta."

"Will you teach me?" she asked anxiously. She took a
handful of his chest hair and twisted it tightly. "Will you
teach me all of them?"

"Tonight?" he asked.

"Will you be staying to be partners with Papa?"

He frowned and asked, "Is that why I'm here in your bed?"

"No," she said, running her tongue up his neck and around his ear. His penis twitched and began to rise as she whispered, "You're here because I want you in my bed, I want you in me—desperately."

And as inexperienced as she was, he thought, she had gotten what she wanted with no problem. What would she be like after tonight? he thought. What would happen to the next poor fool she wanted?

"Are you staying?" she asked again.

"No."

She ran her mouth over his chest, tonguing his nipples, and one hand grasped his semi-erect penis tightly as she said, "Then teach them all to me tonight! I want to learn with you!"

She was a fast learner, too, and damned if the Gunsmith didn't learn a thing or two that night as well.

TWELVE

"Did you sleep well?" Jonathan Braxton asked.

Clint examined Braxton's face for any trace of . . . of what?—of knowledge that the Gunsmith had spent the night educating his daughter in the various ways a man and woman can have sex together.

Carlotta had been an eager student and a model one. She had gone to bed last night an innocent woman/child, and this morning she was woman capable of satisfying her own needs and those of any man—if he could keep up with her.

"Fine," Clint replied, "I slept fine." For all of two hours, he finished to himself.

"Good. You—uh—slept on what we discussed last night, my proposition?"

"I did."

"And?"

"I'll be leaving—" Clint began.

"Wait!" Braxton said. "Let me show you my workshop."

Carlotta looked up at Clint, as if to say I told you so, and smiled.

In spite of himself, Clint was curious about Braxton's

workshop. He was, after all, a legitimate gunsmith.

"All right."

"Good. Take a cup of coffee and come."

Clint poured Tía Maria's excellent coffee into a pewter mug she had given him and carried it with him.

"You will excuse us, my dear," Braxton said to his daughter.

"Of course, Papa."

Braxton led the way to the back of the house where Clint was surprised to find a door that was not made of oak. It was made of metal!

Jonathan Braxton unlocked the door's two locks with two separate keys and then pushed the heavy door open, swinging it inward.

"This room was built here at the back of the house especially for this," Braxton said proudly. "From the outside you can't tell it's here."

Clint followed him inside and then helped him shut the door. When Braxton lit a lamp, the Gunsmith couldn't help but be impressed.

The room ran the length of the house and was about six feet wide. He could barely see what was at the other end, but he was sure it was more of the same: tools, weapons of all kinds—an impressive array of tools to build and tools to kill.

"It must get hot—" Clint began.

"Two of these stones slide out," Braxton said, without pointing them out. "When I'm working with heat for extended periods of time, I remove them for air."

Clint walked around the room, admiring the contents. Hanging on the wall against the house was an array of rifles: Sharps Big Fifty, Winchester '73, older versions of Winchesters, Henrys, Springfields, shotguns, cutdown guns for maximum killing effect at short range, elongated guns for maximum range . . .

And the tools. The finest hand tools for the *finest* work in the most minute detail.

"There's a furnace in the barn, hidden," Braxton said, "and a blacksmith's anvil. I have everything we need here, Clint—"

Clint held up his hand and said, "I have to leave, Jonathan."

"All right, do one thing for me," Braxton said, not one to give up.

"What?" Clint asked.

"Go and do what you have to do, and when you are returning to the United States, come this way. We'll talk again then."

Clint thought about that while Braxton watched him expectantly.

"I can do that," Clint replied.

"Fine," Braxton said, slapping him on the back.

"What kind of volume do you deal in?" Clint asked as they exited the room.

"I'll build *a* gun for *a* man if he pays me enough," Braxton stressed, securing both locks. "At times, I deal in enough to make living near the sea a handy convenience."

That meant ships for pickups and deliveries, and that meant illegal deals as well. Smuggling.

"Some of it's legal," Braxton said, as if reading Clint's mind, "some of it isn't, but it's all profitable, I assure you. Come, let's go back to the dining room."

They returned to the dining room to find Carlotta still sitting there, drinking coffee.

"I sent Paco and some of the men out early this morning. Your friends were still about, but they ran them off a respectable distance. Do they know that you're heading for Mexico City?"

"They shouldn't."

"Good. I'll have Paco and some of the others ride along with you for a while anyway, just in case."

"That's not necessary—" Clint started to protest.

"Nonsense, I insist. I'll also have Tía Maria prepare some food for you to take." Braxton held his hand up to ward off any argument and said, "Please allow me to do this. I haven't had a chance to play a decent game of chess in too long. I owe you for that at least."

"All right," Clint agreed.

Braxton went into the kitchen and as soon as he was out of the room Carlotta jumped up, threw her arms around Clint, and kissed him soundly, passionately, taking his breath away and starting his heart racing.

"Carlotta," he said when he was finally able to pry her free.

"I might not get a chance to say good-bye later," she said, "so I'll do it now."

"It's not good-bye," he said, and he explained the agreement he'd made with her father.

"It's because of me, isn't it?" she asked, standing up and thrusting her proud breasts at him.

"What is?"

"That you're coming back this way."

"Carlotta . . . that's part of it, yes. I'd like to see you again, but don't get the wrong idea."

"You mean marriage?" she asked, giggling. "Wouldn't that surprise Papa?"

Not only Papa . . . Clint thought.

"No, I'm not getting a wrong idea, Clint," she said, taking her seat again. "Just all the right ones."

Braxton and Carlotta walked Clint outside where Paco had Duke saddled and waiting. He turned and shook hands with Jonathan Braxton, an interesting man whom he wished he had more time to get to know. And Carlotta, an interesting young woman whom he knew very well after one night—but one that he would fondly remember and perhaps anticipate repeating.

He was curious to see what he had wrought.

"Remember," Braxton said as Clint mounted up, "you're coming back this way."

"I'll remember," Clint said. "Until then, be careful who you do business with."

"I am always careful," Braxton said, "that they have enough money before I decide to do business with them. Safe journey, Clint. I hope you find what you're looking for."

"Ready, *señor*?" Paco asked.

"Ready, Paco."

He pulled Duke's head around and he, Paco, and three other men started south along the beach.

They stayed with him for a few hours, the other three men riding behind Clint and Paco, who spoke only infrequently.

"Paco, have you worked for Mr. Braxton for very long?" Clint asked at one point.

"Not long," Paco said. "Only since he moved into this house and set up his . . . business."

"How do you feel about the upcoming revolution?"

"Revolutions come and go," Paco said. "The important thing is to make money from them while they are here."

Clint was sure he could hear Jonathan Braxton talking there.

Later Paco asked, "You are a very famous American, are you not, *señor*?"

"I'm afraid that might be true."

"Could you not turn your fame into a fortune?" Paco asked, curious.

"I suppose I could, Paco, if I wanted to put myself on display—which I don't."

Paco couldn't seem to understand that, and Clint was beginning to think that maybe the Mexican had worked for Braxton *too* long.

Finally, Paco pulled his pony to a halt and said, "You must travel west from here, *señor*, to reach Mexico City."

"Thank you for riding with me, Paco."

Paco was staring intently at Clint and finally asked, "Did the *padrino* offer you a partnership, *señor*?"

"He did. Why?"

"Did you accept?"

"I didn't."

"You do not want to be rich?"

"That's never been a big ambition of mine."

Paco shook his head and said, "I have not known many Americans, *señor*, and they have all been crazy."

"And I'm no different, right?"

"You, *señor*," Paco said, "are possibly the craziest of all. *Adiós*."

"*Adiós*, Paco."

Clint watched the Mexicans ride away and thought that Paco had probably come to the right conclusion for the wrong reason.

Any man who went ghost hunting had to be crazy, and Paco had missed that completely.

THIRTEEN

The man with the red sash didn't have the sash on now. In fact, he wasn't wearing anything. When he had sex with a woman he preferred to do it naked. His guns, of course, were very close at hand.

The woman next to him was a rebel. She was by no means beautiful, but she was solidly built, and he liked his women solidly built, with heavy breasts, hips, thighs, and buttocks.

"Have you decided, Señor Bill—"

"Butler," the man said, correcting her, "the name you call me by is James Butler."

"Señor James," she said, immediately contrite, "my brother, he wants to know if you have decided to join us in our fight to reach the capital."

"I don't know," the man called Butler said.

"You would be paid much money, *señor*."

"I don't need much money, Delores."

"I would also be part of the bargain, *señor*," she reminded him. "As long as you are a rebel, I will be your woman."

"I wouldn't *be* a rebel, Delores," James Butler corrected her, "I'd be *working* for rebels. There's a difference. I don't have any stock in who lives in the President's house."

"You do not care about money or about who rules my country," Delores said. "What do you care about, *señor*?"

"If I knew that, Delores," Butler said, reaching for her, "I don't suppose I'd be here in this little town."

They were in the town of Acambaro, whose name Butler did not know the meaning of, nor did he want to. He wondered how a woman could believe a man who said he didn't care about money.

James Butler did intend to work for the rebels, but he intended to make them so grateful to him for agreeing to do so that they'd pay him almost anything he asked. Making them wait was part of that plan.

And having Delores down between his legs, busily working on him with her mouth and her tongue, was part of the deal, too. She claimed—and the rebel leader claimed—that she was the man's sister, but Butler knew differently.

He knew that she was the bandit's wife, and that was how desperate the rebels were to have James Butler Hickok on their side.

Outside of Acambaro was a rebel—or bandit—hideout, depending on who you were and how you looked at it. The bandits preferred to think of themselves as rebels. The *federalistas* preferred to think of the rebels as bandits.

"I do not think I could sit out here," one of the rebels said to some of his compadres, "while I knew that my wife was in town with some gringo fucking her."

"Chico," a voice said behind him. Chico's shoulders

tensed as his friends looked behind him, and finally he
himself turned to find the rebel leader standing behind
him.

His name was Benito. It was not his real name, but he
took it for Benito Juárez, who he felt was a great leader
and a great president.

"Delores is one of us," Benito said. "She is a rebel
fighting for the same cause you and I are, only she is
fighting in a different way. Do you understand?"

"*Sí*, Benito."

Benito walked right up to Chico until there was barely
room between them for light to pass. Chico was five feet
ten and had to crane his neck to look at Benito's face.

"Once we are in the President's Palace," he said, "we
will have no more need for the gringo. Right now, his
reputation as a walking dead man will only help gain us
support. Afterward, we will see to it that the dead man
walks no more."

"*Sí*, Benito."

"And you, Chico, could find yourself joining him if
you do not control your tongue."

"S—*sí*, Benito," Chico stammered, "as you say."

"Always," Benito said, sharply jabbing Chico's chest
with a forefinger, "remember that it is always as I say."

"Wake up!" James Butler shouted, slapping Delores
hard on the rump.

"Ow!" she cried out, staring at him darkly from over
her shoulder.

The only reason she put up with this gringo and his
sexual appetite was because her husband, Benito—soon
to be Presidente Benito—promised her that when they had
reached the President's Palace she would be among the

firing squad that killed him. Until then . . .

"Now, you cow, raise it up," Butler said.

He didn't like women with firm ass cheeks; He preferred women like Delores, whose big ass was almost like butter.

"Now!" he said.

"Get dressed," he said later, climbing out of the bed.

"What for?" she asked. "Where are we going?"

"It's time to ride out and talk to your—uh—brother about our deal."

"You've decided to join us?"

"I've decided," he said, pulling on his pants, "to let your people hire me."

At last, she thought, sliding to the edge of the bed and reaching for her clothes. Perhaps this would signal an end to her having to submit herself to his every sexual whim. Even Benito—who admittedly was an animal—was not as disgusting in bed as this man. Her husband simply took his pleasure and then left her alone, which was how she preferred her sex.

"That's wonderful," she said, trying to sound enthusiastic.

"Sure it is," he said, buttoning his shirt. Then he reached for his sash and guns.

The man who called himself James Butler laughed to himself at this whore and her husband, both of whom thought that he was willing to help put an illiterate in the President's Palace. He was willing to help, all right, he thought, winding the red sash behind him and then inserting the .32s . . . help himself to all the money or gold they had in their war chest to pay for their pathetic little revolution.

And he'd kill anyone who got in his way.

As James Butler and Delores rode out of town to the west, Clint Adams rode into town from the east, missing them by scant moments.

It was not time for the Gunsmith to find his ghost, yet.

FOURTEEN

Clint found a run-down stable at the end of Acambaro's single street and had to wake the liveryman in order to get a stall for Duke.

"Take good care of him," Clint said firmly.

"What I look like?" the elderly man demanded sleepily. "I give you a stall; you take care of him yourself."

Clint was about to object—forcefully—when he decided that it would probably be better for the big gelding if he did see to him on his own. He took the saddle off, rubbed him down, and saw that he had enough grain. Then he went in search of a cantina. It had been a rough two-day ride from the Gulf to Acambaro, and he needed a drink.

Acambaro had one of everything. A single street, one livery stable, and one cantina/hotel. On his way there he passed the sheriff's office, but he decided not to stop in and announce his presence this time. If Hickok—or the imposter—were in town, he wouldn't want to let him know that he was there as well.

Not yet, anyway.

He entered the cantina and found it empty but for a man

behind the bar and a man half-sprawled on one of the four square tables.

"*Señor*?" the fat bartender asked, looking bored.

"Do you have beer?"

"*Sí*, but it is warm."

"Whiskey?"

"*Sí*."

"Give me a glass and the bottle."

"As you wish, *señor*."

The bartender set a shot glass on the bar with a bottle of rot gut, and Clint decided that he would risk two glasses. The first he took to cut the dust, and the second he took for good measure.

He finished the second drink, closed the bottle, returned it to the bartender, and flipped a coin onto the bar. As the fat man looked at the coin, Clint looked at him expectantly.

"*Señor*," the man said, mournfully, "I cannot change that."

"You won't have to if you answer a question."

The man shrugged and said suspiciously, "That does not sound very hard, *señor*."

"I'm looking for a man."

"I could get you a woman, *señor*," the man said, leering now, "very easily—"

"I'm looking for a friend of mine who might have been in town recently."

"Pardon, *señor*," the man said, actually looking embarrassed.

"He's a tall man; he'd have long blond hair, a big mustache, and he wears a red sash around his waist with his guns in it. The guns might be worn at an odd angle—" He stopped short when he saw that no further description was necessary.

"That one!" the bartender breathed.

"He's been here?"

"He has been here for a week or more, *señor*, in a room upstairs."

"Which room?" Clint asked, starting for the stairs.

"He is not there now, *señor*. He left not a half hour ago with a woman."

"What woman?"

"A—how do you say—large woman," the man said, illustrating his point with his hands. "Big in the chest and the behind."

"Where were they going?"

"This I do not know, *señor*."

"Tell me what you do know."

"He came here with the woman and some men. They drank. The men left; this man and the woman stay and take a room upstairs."

"What were they doing?"

The bartender grinned and said, "The floors and ceiling are very thin, *señor*, and they . . . appreciated each other so much that one could hear the bed moving against the floor." The man put one hand on top of the other and said, "How do you call it? The two-backed beast?"

"The beast with two backs."

"*Sí*, that is it."

"All this time?"

"Amazing, no?" the man asked. "They stopped at times for whiskey and food, but most of the time they make like this beast."

The man reached for the coin now and Clint covered it with the tip of his right forefinger.

"Which way did they go when they left town?"

"*Señor*, this I do not know."

"I shouldn't even have asked," Clint said, removing

his finger from the coin, which disappeared in a split second. He realized that the town had one road and he had ridden in from the east. They had to have ridden to the west, toward Mexico City—unless they didn't take the road at all.

"All right, the coin is yours."

"*Gracias, señor.*"

Clint started for the door and the bartender called out, "*Señor?*"

"Yes."

"Was this man who they say he was?"

"Who are they?"

"People," the man said, shrugging.

"And who did they say this man was?"

"They say that the man is the ghost of the famous Wild Bill Hickok, a man who is dead. Could this be so?"

"I don't believe in ghosts, bartender," Clint said and left the cantina.

Outside, as he walked to the livery to retrieve Duke, he thought ghosts don't have sex.

Do they?

The ground was hard around Acambaro, and the Gunsmith was the first to admit that he was not an expert tracker. Obvious trails he was able to follow, even those that had been deliberately covered up, but this was different. No attempt had been made to cover this trail because the ground did that without knowing it.

He sat astride Duke, to whom he had apologized for putting his saddle back on so soon. He stared at the hard-baked ground, waiting for it to tell him something, but it remained uncooperative. He removed his hat and drew his sleeve across his sweating brow.

"All right, Duke," Clint said. "I think our only choice

is to stay on this road and, if we don't pick up a trail, just keep going to Mexico City. This man—this ghost—will end up there.''

Firmly replacing his hat he added, ''I can feel it!''

FIFTEEN

Mexico City was impressive.

Although it couldn't match San Francisco or, perhaps, some of the other, larger cities of the United States, it had a grandeur that could not be denied.

Clint found a livery stable with an eager boy at work and, dismounting, asked the boy some questions.

"How far are we from the President's Palace?"

"Oh, *señor*, we are across the city from *El Presidente*'s home," the boy replied.

"Could you give me directions to a stable that would be closer?"

The boy looked sad, either at losing the business or losing the chance to get his hands on Duke, whose presence had doubled the size of the boy's eyes. Clint compensated by tossing the boy a coin, which he deftly caught, and then he gave Clint the directions he'd asked for.

Following those directions, Clint found the other livery, which was housed in a brick building and run in a more businesslike manner, probably due to its proximity to the President's Palace.

Clint handed Duke over to a man who called to one of his grooms and told him to take special care of this animal—this without first hearing it from Clint. The Gunsmith felt secure about Duke's care and asked for directions to a good but not too expensive hotel.

He entered the lobby of the Hotel de Jesús, a four-story, adobe building that was probably cheaper than some of the others that might have been constructed of brick. This one, however, managed to match the city's grandeur, if to a somewhat faded degree.

"A room, please."

"Of course, *señor*," the clerk said. "How long will you be staying with us?"

"I'm not sure," Clint said, signing the register. "A few days, maybe a week."

"Do you need assistance to your room?"

"No," Clint said, "I can handle it."

"Enjoy your stay."

"I'll try," Clint responded.

His room was on the second floor of the structure, a corner room just off the main street. He dumped his saddlebags on the bed and went to the window to look out. He thought he might be able to see the President's Palace from there, but he could not. Neither could he see much of the main street. He had a clear view of the side street, but the building across the way was three stories high, and all he could see of the main street was a small patch.

He went back to the bed to sit down and figure out his next move. Weeks of traveling had brought him this far, and now that he was here—and Mexico City was larger than he had expected—where was he to look?

He tried to reason it out, and some of the events of the past days helped him to put it together, specifically the fact that the Sheriff's brother in Nuevo Laredo had assumed that, with his reputation, he was sure to have been recruited by the rebels as a mercenary.

If the rumors of Wild Bill Hickok's presence in Mexico had spread to the United States, then it stood to reason that Mexicans knew of it. That meant the rebels knew as well, and what rebel force could resist trying to recruit a famous gunman who was supposed to be dead?

Since many Mexicans were very superstitious people, the rebels, with a "walking dead man," who was also a legend, on their side, would command instant support from many of the people. Whether the man was Hickok or not, the rebels wouldn't be able to resist that.

He got up and walked back to the window, drawing the lacy curtain aside. It was really very simple when you thought about it. Find the rebels, and he'd find the man who was calling himself Wild Bill Hickok.

Now all that remained was to figure out a way to get in touch with the rebels. Of course, the simplest way to do that was to sit back and wait for them to find him.

For one of the few times in his life, Clint Adams was going to trade off his reputation as the Gunsmith. All he had to do was let it be known that he was in Mexico City—and available—and they were sure to try to recruit him—even if they already had Hickok on their side.

Two legends were better than one, he thought, scowling at the notion. He didn't like referring to himself as a legend—he didn't *feel* very legendary—but he had to admit that some people regarded him that way.

He walked to a pitcher and basin on the chest of drawers by the window and found the basin full of water. The hotel afforded their guests excellent service. It was lukewarm, but he didn't want to drink it, so that didn't matter. He removed his hat and shirt and proceeded to wash as much of himself as he could. As he was doing so, he suddenly had an idea about how he could get word to the rebels that the Gunsmith was in town, and it would require more than a quick basin bath.

He put on a fresh shirt, replaced his hat, and went downstairs to talk to the desk clerk.

"Excuse me," he said.

The man turned from the work he was doing—filling pigeonholes with envelopes, it looked like—and said, "*Sí, señor*, how may I serve you."

"I've been on the trail a long time," Clint said, "and I'm lonely."

The man looked at him and Clint suddenly realized that he'd phrased that wrong.

"For female companionship," he added hastily.

The man's look of interest faded and he said, "Of course."

"Do you know someplace where I can go?"

"A cantina, *señor*," the man said, impatient now. "There are many women—"

"I want the best," Clint said, taking out a dollar bill and showing it to the man.

"Ah, yes," the man said. He closed his thumb and forefinger over one end of the bill, but Clint held onto the other end.

"Two-one-four, Avenida Valencia."

"Directions, please."

The man gave him the directions and Clint released his hold on the money.

"You may tell them that Ignacio sent you."

"Thanks, Ignacio," Clint said. "Now I would like to use your bath facilities."

"That would be advisable, *señor*," the man agreed. "We could have a tub placed in your room—"

"That won't be necessary—"

"In that case if you go out the front door, make a right, and walk to the next street—the one alongside the hotel—you will find a public bathhouse."

His tone clearly said that only a cretin would use a public bathhouse, but then Clint wasn't looking to make an impression on a lowly desk clerk.

"Thank you."

He went to the bathhouse and took a hot bath that turned out to be longer than he'd intended because the hot water felt so good. After that he found his way to the house located on Avenida Valencia.

The building was a three-story brick structure with no sign outside to indicate what kind of an establishment it was. That probably meant that everybody already knew what kind of place it was. It would probably be frequented by *federales* and rebels alike, and that was the general idea.

SIXTEEN

Clint tried the twin front doors and found one of them open. He walked in and found himself in a rather plain entry hall. If this was a cathouse, it was unlike any other he'd ever been in. Most of them went for opulence in their furnishings, and this place just did not fit the bill.

Never one to pay for his pleasures, he'd already decided that he'd have to make an exception this time. His intention was to pay for a girl, spend some time with her—after all, he didn't intend to waste his money—and brag about what a deadly gunman and living legend he was. The first time that same girl was with a rebel, she was sure to tell him about it. Of course, it worked the other way, too; the first time she spent time with a *federale*—but that was a chance he'd have to take.

He closed the door behind him and studied the foyer he stood in. There were doors on either side of him, and as he was wondering which one to approach, the one on the right slid open and a woman stepped out.

She didn't look like any whorehouse madam he'd ever met before. In fact, she looked enough like Tía Maria to be her sister.

"*Señor*?" she said, approaching him. She was dressed in a shapeless, plain dress which, of course, was only shapeless because she was wearing it. "Can I help you?"

"Uh—I may be in the wrong place, but—"

"What is it you wish?"

Clint turned several answers over in his mind, then decided to go with directness and said, "A woman."

"*Sí*?" she said, her face expressionless. "And who sent you here?"

"Ignacio, at the hotel—"

"I know where he is from," she said, cutting him off. The woman looked extremely bored with her lot in life. "Here you do not get a choice, like in *los Estados Unidos*. Here, you must take what you get, whoever is available."

He frowned—like a dissatisfied customer, he hoped—and asked, "What if I don't like what I get?"

"You will," she said with absolute certainty.

"I mean, what if I like blondes and I get a redhead, or—"

"After a few moments," she said, folding her arms across her chest, "you won't care about hair color."

Her look dared him to deny it.

"Well, I'll tell you what," Clint said, "if I don't enjoy myself, I won't come back."

She shrugged.

"And I won't send my friends."

She shrugged.

He put his hand in his pocket to bring out some money and she said, "You pay upstairs."

"Fine. Where upstairs?"

"Room number six."

"*Gracias.*"

She waved a hand at him impatiently and went back

through the sliding door, closing it behind her. He wondered idly how she had known he was there, and then he went up the stairs to the second floor.

As he reached the head of the stairs, he was looking at room number three. He looked right, then left before spotting number six. He walked up to the door and knocked.

A lovely girl with long black hair answered, looked at him, and said, "*Qué lindo*."

"I like you, too," he said, looking down at her. She was about five feet two, wearing a nightgown so sheer that were it not for the furry fringe he might not have been able to tell she was wearing one. Her breasts were small, her nipples dark, and she smelled of some kind of perfume that was probably supposed to be exotic, but was overpowering instead. Still, she was a tasty looking morsel, as small women went.

"Would you like to come in?"

"Of course."

She stepped away from the door to allow him to enter, then shut it, and put her back against it. The room was sparsely furnished with a plain chest of drawers and a equally plain bed. The mattress, however, was thick and full and he knew it would be comfortable. The money this particular whorehouse made obviously went into the comfort of its customers—good mattresses and better women.

"A gringo?" she asked timidly.

"I'm afraid so," he said. "Do you have anything against gringos?"

She grinned, moved close to him, and pressed her body up against him.

"Just this."

"That's good enough," he said. He reached down to

grasp the bottom of her nightgown. "May I?"

She took a step back, batted her eyes at him, and said, "*Por favor.*"

To make it easy for him she lifted her arms, and her little breasts lifted also. He tugged the nightgown up and over her head, dropping it to the ground. He placed his hands against her chest with his thumbs on her nipples, and she closed her eyes and moaned.

"What's your name?"

"Apasionata."

He stared at her and said. "I'll ask you for one thing. I don't want any whore games or whore names. Do you understand?"

"I understand, *señor*," she said, looking kittenish. With her size, and her slightly slanted eyes, it was a look she didn't have to put on.

"All right," he said. He palmed her breasts as her nipples swelled and poked at his hands.

"What's your real name?"

"Raquel."

"Why the phony one?"

She shrugged. "Some men say it sounds—how do you say—"

"Sensual?" he finished.

"*Sí*. Sensual."

"I like Raquel."

She grinned and said, "Raquel likes you," and reached for his crotch.

"No whore games, Raquel," he warned her. "Do you know who I am?"

"No, *señor*?"

"I am a very famous man."

"Famous?" she asked, her eyes widening. "Are you *el Presidente de los Estados Unidos*?"

He laughed and said, "No, I'm not the President of the United States. I am even more famous than he is."

"Ooh, tell me, who you are," she said, clapping her hands together in unsuppressed glee.

"My name is Clint Adams," he said. When he saw that the name did not register with her, he said, "Some people call me the Gunsmith."

"Ah!" she said, putting her hands over her. "The notorious *Americano* gunman!"

"Right."

"*Señor*," she said, "I am growing hotter with each passing moment." He didn't need to be told that; he could smell her readiness.

He lifted her up in his arms, carried her to the bed, and placed her gently on it. He undressed while she watched, and she smiled in glee again when she saw his cock standing at full readiness.

Since his original cause for visiting this place had been business, he decided to get pleasure out of the way quickly. She *was* attractive, but he detested the idea of paying for sex, and her perfume was giving him a headache.

He climbed onto the bed and mounted her, seeking nothing but his own release so he could leave. Raquel, on the other hand, seemed to be enjoying herself immensely, and the harder he drove into her, the louder and longer she squealed. Whores weren't supposed to have orgasms with their customers, but this one obviously had not read the rules and in moments she was writhing beneath him in the throes of one. He exploded inside her before her orgasm had subsided, and as he filled her, she went right into another climax, longer than the one before.

"Aye, my Gunsmith," she whispered, and he knew that he had accomplished what he had come to do.

She'd be talking about this to everyone for days—maybe weeks and months—to come.

"You will come back soon?" she asked, watching him while he dressed.

"I'll come back," he told her, and then he decided to make one more attempt to make sure that she talked to people about him, "but you must promise me something, Raquel."

"What?" she asked. She was sitting on the bed, propped up on her elbows.

"Don't tell anyone that I was here," he said, and he could see her eyes begin to glow. Tell a woman *not* to say something, and she was sure to say it, he figured.

"I will not," she promised.

"Good."

Feeling he had accomplished what he'd come to, he settled up with her and left, eager to get outside and breathe some fresh air to drive the scent of her overpowering perfume from his nostrils.

SEVENTEEN

It took four days, and Clint wondered how many men Raquel—otherwise known as Apasionata—had to go through before her words reached the right one.

He'd seen as much of Mexico City as he could, although the whole point of walking as far as he could in each direction was to *be* seen. He'd begun to think that he should have told the girl what hotel he was staying in, but any interested party could have found that out easy enough from the shapeless madam, and he hadn't wanted to make his ploy too obvious.

He was having breakfast in a cantina near his hotel when they walked in. He didn't pay any attention to them at first, except for the woman. She had dark hair, cut very short, almost like a man's, but it was definitely a woman's body inside the jeans and shirt she was wearing. The thrust of her breasts was . . . challenging, for want of a better word.

The man with her was young, in his twenties—a little younger than the woman, probably—and he was of medium height and build. Clint had the feeling that he'd be no match for the woman, in bed or out, and wondered if he'd ever have the chance.

He turned his attention back to his breakfast, but from the corner of his eye he could see them approaching his table, and he hoped that contact was finally about to be made.

"*Señor*?" It was the man's voice, and he sounded unsure of himself.

He looked up and saw them both looking at him, the man somewhat timidly and the woman boldly.

"Can I help you?" he asked, with his eyes on the woman.

"You are Señor Clint Adams?"

"That's right."

"W—we would like to speak to you, *señor*," the man said, "if it is permissible."

Clint saw the expression of disgust on the woman's face and knew she'd had enough.

"Manuel," she said.

"*Sí*?"

"Go outside and wait."

"But—"

"Outside!" the woman hissed, and the man jumped and then turned and hurried outside.

The woman pulled out the chair opposite the Gunsmith and sat down. He decided, examining her up close, that she had a mouth that was made for kissing, with the upper and lower lips equally full; but the set of it was too grim.

He continued to eat, waiting for her to speak.

"Señor Adams."

"Yes."

"You are called the Gunsmith?"

He looked at her then and said, "Would you like some coffee?"

She looked as if she were going to refuse and then changed her mind.

"Yes, please," she said.

Her English was good, he reflected, as he poured her a cup, but she appeared to be Mexican. He thought that her hair must've been luxurious when it was long.

"What's your name?" he asked her.

"Victoria."

"That's a pretty name."

"How pretty my name is is of no importance," she said abruptly.

"What is, then?"

"We would like to talk to you," she said. There were no diners at the other tables immediately near them, but she had lowered her voice as if there were.

"Who would?"

"I speak for . . . the rebels."

"The rebels?" he asked, feigning ignorance.

He continued eating and she said, "You do know about the upcoming revolution?"

"I've heard rumors."

"We are looking for men."

"Mercenaries?" he inquired.

"Yes," she said, "but you would not be a mercenary, Señor Adams. You are, after all, the Gunsmith."

He looked directly at her and asked, "How did you know I was in town."

"Manuel, he heard from a girl—a *puta*."

"A what?"

"A whore," she said.

"Oh."

She looked at him boldly again and said, "You do not look like a man who would pay for sex."

"I'm not."

She frowned and said, "But—"

"I heard about the revolution, Victoria," he said, finishing the last of his breakfast. He looked at her and said, "I heard that there was money to be made."

"There . . . could be, yes."

"I didn't know how to contact any of the rebels, but I figured out a way . . . didn't I?"

She studied him for a moment and he was sure she almost smiled.

"Yes, you did."

"Who do I talk to?"

"Benito."

"Where is he?"

"Not in the city."

"When will he get back?"

"I do not know. When he does I will let you know. He will be eager to talk to you."

"To tell you the truth, Victoria," he said, "I'd much rather talk to you."

She didn't know how to react to that, so she lifted her coffee cup and sipped from it.

"What are you supposed to be doing today?" he asked her.

She shrugged and said, "I have nothing planned."

"Would you show me your city?"

"It is not my city—our city—yet," she said grimly, "but it will be soon."

"You have a lovely mouth."

She stared at him and then said, "I do not know how to . . . act when you talk that way."

"Smile," he suggested. "Your mouth is made for smiles and kisses, not grimness."

She touched her lips and said, "Does my mouth look grim?"

"It does."

She kept touching it, thinking.

"Why don't you send Manuel away and show me your city? He's not your man, is he?"

"Manuel?" she asked, looking disgusted again.

"Then send him away."

She put her coffee cup down and nodded.

"I will send him away."

"I'll pay for my breakfast and meet you outside."

"All right."

She rose and he watched her walk toward the door, admiring the way her firm buttocks moved when she walked. She was a tall woman, about five feet ten or so and full-bodied.

Waiting for contact had been tedious. Waiting for this Benito, though, now that contact had been made might not be unpleasant at all.

"When do we leave for Mexico City?" James Butler asked the bandit leader, Benito, who fancied himself a rebel leader.

"Soon," Benito said.

They were at a camp that was between Acambaro and Mexico City, and they had been there for some time. Butler didn't relish sleeping on the hard-packed ground with a bunch of Mexicans. He'd would rather have been in a hotel in Mexico City, in bed with Delores, Benito's wife. She was at the campfire now, bent over while preparing food for the men, and he admired her wide buttocks as they strained against the fabric of her jeans. A woman with a butt like that, he thought, shouldn't really wear jeans. She shouldn't wear anything at all. He wondered idly what Benito would say if he suggested that to him.

"Have you got enough in your war chest to finance this little revolution?"

Benito looked at Butler and said, "There will be enough to pay you, Señor Hick—I mean, Butler."

"Oh, there'll be enough for me, all right, Butler thought. As soon as I find out where your cache is, there'll be plenty for me.

Like all of it.

EIGHTEEN

Victoria showed Clint some of Mexico City he would not have seen otherwise—like her bedroom.

They started out on a tour and she took him to where he could see the President's Palace.

"That is where Benito will soon be," she said proudly.

"And will you be El Presidente's First Lady?"

She looked at him and said, "Benito is married; he has a first lady."

Her face was unreadable. He couldn't tell if she had feelings of regret about that.

"Do you have a man, Victoria?" he asked. "A woman as beautiful as you must have someone."

"No," she said, shaking her head. "No one."

He reached up to cup her chin, to run his thumb first over her upper lip and then the lower one.

"You have a lovely mouth."

"You flatter me, Clint."

"I'm telling you the truth, that's all," he said, and then right there, in the shade of the President's Palace, he leaned over and kissed her. Her lips didn't move, but neither did she pull away. Even so, he enjoyed the way her mouth felt against his.

"Why did you do that?" she asked.

"Because I desire you," he said. "I have since you first walked into the cantina."

She frowned and said, "You did not see us when we first entered the cantina."

"Yes," he said, "I did."

She frowned at him again, studying him, and they walked on.

She showed him a house where she said Maximilian kept a woman; she showed him a beautiful church, the Church of Santa Maria, she called it. She showed him the federale garrisons; she took him to another cantina for lunch, a place where she was known very well, and then she asked him if there was somewhere he wanted to see.

"Yes."

"Where?"

"Where you live."

She stared at him.

"Do you live alone?"

"Yes."

"You're not ashamed of where you live, are you?"

She shrugged and said, "It is a room."

"I'd like to see it."

"Very well."

As she led the way there, he asked, "Does Benito give you the authority to recruit new people like this?"

"No," she said, "not precisely—but when he meets you, I don't think he'll mind."

They walked to a part of the city that was not even remotely in the shadow of the palace. It was a poor section, where children ran up to them begging for coins and old people lay in the streets begging for scraps.

"You live here?"

"It is what I can afford."

She took him to an adobe building with a small general store on the first floor.

"I have a room above," she said, taking him to a side door. She opened the door with a key and led him up a flight of stairs and into her room.

There was a sagging bed, a pitted and scarred wooden dresser, a straight-backed wooden chair with a crooked leg, and a crucifix on the wall.

"It is not much," she admitted.

"It becomes more when you enter it," he said.

She turned to face him and asked, "Why do you say things like that?"

"I told you before," he said, moving closer and taking her by the shoulders. She had wide shoulders for a woman, but they had an impressive pair of breasts to support and did a splendid job. "I want you."

"We have just met."

"That doesn't matter. Rarely have I met a woman with your presence, with your type of beauty."

"What type is that?"

"Proud." He put one hand behind her neck and touched her hair. "Your hair must have been beautiful when it was long."

"What makes you think it was ever long?"

"It had to be," he said, caressing the back of her neck.

She closed her eyes and leaned back against the pressure of his hand.

"It was."

He leaned forward and kissed her full lips again. This time they stirred beneath his and she leaned into him. He slid his hand down from the back of her neck to the small of her back and pulled her to him so that her breasts were pressed against him. She wasn't wearing anything under the shirt and he could feel her hard nipples digging into his chest.

He pulled his mouth away from hers, but only an inch or so, and it was she who instituted the kiss this time. Her mouth moved against his and then opened and her tongue flicked out tentatively.

He put his other arm around her now and she brought hers up around his neck. Now they were kissing hungrily, grinding their bodies together, and he wondered if she was giving in to him simply to entertain him until her leader, Benito, showed up. Even if that were the case, it had gone too far now to stop. He was excited, his erection throbbing in his jeans, and he wanted to feel her bare breasts in his hands, her nipples against his palms and his mouth.

She was a big woman and she filled his arms. He slid his hands farther down her back to cup her firm buttocks, then slid them up again, this time beneath her shirt to run his fingers over her bare back. Her skin was smooth and warm to his touch.

The kiss went on until it seemed pointless to continue. There were other ways to show how much they wanted each other—whatever the reason.

"Will that bed hold the two of us?" he asked, starting to unbutton her shirt, beginning at the bottom.

"We will find out," she said as she let him undress her . . .

● ● ●

"It is demeaning."

"What is?" he asked, frowning.

She was lying on her left side, facing away from him, and he had been admiring the strong, graceful lines of her back.

"Losing control."

"Victoria—" he said, touching her shoulder, but she jerked it away from him.

"There is a revolution to be won," she said, "and I should not be indulging in . . . animal pleasures."

"Animal pleasures?"

He reached for her shoulder again and this time he didn't let her pull away. Instead, he pulled her over so that she was lying on her back. Her firm breasts flattened out very slightly for their size.

"Victoria, you can't be sorry for what we did here between us."

She stared at him. "I don't want to . . ." she said, helplessly.

"There is nothing wrong with enjoying being with a man."

"But . . . but I lose control . . ."

"There's nothing wrong with that, either," he said. "Victoria, you make a man feel like he's something very special. That's a beautiful thing to do."

She looked up at him with tears in her eyes and she said, "But you are special. You made . . . things happen to me that I . . . I couldn't control. I have been with many men, Clint," she said. "I am not a saint, but it has never been like this before."

He put his hand over one of her breasts and she closed her eyes and caught her breath. Her nipple began to swell beneath his palm.

"I can't help it," she said and turning to him she

eagerly sought his mouth with her own.

"Don't try," he said.

They went out to dinner afterward, and then Clint asked Victoria to go back to his room with him.

"Why?" she asked, regarding him coolly. The passionate, uncontrollable woman that she was in bed disappeared when she got dressed, but now he knew she was there, smoldering just below the surface.

"The bed in my room is stronger," he said.

NINETEEN

For two days it went on like that, and once or twice Clint caught sight of Manuel glowering at them from a doorway across some street. He found out very little from Victoria about the revolution or about herself, beyond the fact that her full name was Victoria Maria Elena Pendencia.

"Does he love you?" he asked her. They were in a cantina and Manuel was in a doorway across the way.

She shrugged.

"I do not know," she said. "I cannot be concerned with love."

"Only pleasure, huh?"

She glared at him and then said, "I am simply staying with you until Benito arrives."

"Sure."

"When he does, the revolution will be at hand."

"What are you going to do? Storm the palace? Instant revolution?"

"That will be up to Benito. He will tell us what he wants us to do."

"Will he also tell me how much money I'll make?"

115

"You should not be concerned with money."

"I know," he said, "but it's a flaw of mine. I can't help it."

"Sometimes," she said, staring at him with a puzzled frown, "I do not understand you."

"When that happens tell me," he said, "and I'll try to explain."

"When we are making love you are gentle, even loving."

He reached across to place his hand over hers and said, "You make it easy, Victoria."

"You see?" she said, pulling her hand away from his. "And then you say things like that to me. A man who can talk as sweet and be as loving as you are does not seem the type of man to be a mercenary."

He shrugged helplessly and said, "A man has to make a living, my love."

"I am not your love," she said, and the idea seemed to annoy her. That is, either the idea that she was—or she wasn't—he couldn't tell which.

"You could be," he said, looking at her mouth. Her mouth interested him even more than her breasts. She knew how to use it expertly, but even when it was set as grimly as it was now, it excited him.

"Victoria—"

"Don't say something sweet to me again," she snapped.

She stood up and he asked, "Where are you going?"

"I want to talk to Manuel, and see if Benito has reached the city yet."

"Will I see you later?"

"I do not know," she said haughtily—but she didn't walk out right away.

"I'll be at my hotel for dinner," he said. "Join me there, and then we'll go to my room."

"Benito—"

"If Benito is in town, bring him with you. I'll buy him dinner—and then you and I will go to my room."

"When Benito is here I will not be able—" she began, but then she stopped and simply said, "I will see you later, Clint."

"I'll count the hours."

She gave him a look of pure exasperation and stormed out. He finished his coffee, paid, and left the café. Manuel was gone from his latest doorway.

Clint went back to his hotel, walking so that he had to pass the President's Palace. It was a grand residence, all right, but he wondered why, whenever the leader of some revolution managed to win his way inside, he suddenly forgot the reasons he'd been fighting to get there.

TWENTY

"Where are you going?" James Butler demanded of Benito. He had seen the man mounting his horse and hurried to find out what was happening.

"I am riding into Mexico City."

"Wait a minute and I'll ride in with you," Butler said.

"No," Benito said. He turned to face squarely the man with the red sash. Aware that he was talking to an American legend, he nevertheless felt that, as leader of the revolution, he had every right to expect to be obeyed, even by such a man.

"We are paying you, *señor*," he said, "so I expect you to abide by my decisions."

"And what decision is this?"

"We have people in the city," Benito said. "We are arranging to buy guns and I must speak to my people. If you were to be seen in the capital with me, it would not do."

"So you want me to stay here and rot."

Benito looked past Butler and the man turned to see what the rebel leader was looking at. Delores was stand-

119

ing in front of the cave Benito used as his headquarters and his sleeping quarters. She was wearing a skirt now, and he could see her sturdy legs and large breasts. With Benito gone from camp . . .

"You may use my quarters," Benito said, "while I am gone."

Butler wasted no time. As soon as Benito left, he grabbed Delores and pulled her into the cave. The other rebels watched, but knew that they could do nothing. Their leader—and his wife—were making great sacrifices for the cause.

Inside the cave Butler pushed Delores down on the pallet Benito used as a bed.

"Tell me about the money," he said as she tried to pick herself up off the bed.

"What do you mean?"

"I'm worried," he said as she sat on the pallet.

"About what?"

"About being paid."

"There is plenty of money—"

"But Benito said he has to buy guns," Butler said. "That costs money."

"There is enough," she insisted.

"How do I know?"

"Benito says—"

"I'd like to see for myself," Butler said, as he put his sash and guns on a wooden table in the center of the cavern, which was lit by a small fire on the floor. He could see her eyes flick to his guns, and he knew she'd like to kill him.

He also knew she wouldn't try.

"You will have to ask Benito," she said. "He is the

only one who knows where the money is."

"Is it all money?" he asked.

"I don't understand—"

"Cash, is it all cash, or are there other things?"

"There is gold, and silver—" she said. Then she stopped and said, "You will have to ask Benito."

"All right," he said. He walked to her and took her solid breasts in his hands. "I'll ask Benito."

Benito was not happy—for several reasons.

Number one, he was in Mexico City while he was sure James Butler was abusing his wife, Delores, back at the camp. Delores was a good wife and an even better soldier of the revolution.

The second reason was that while in his room in Mexico City, not far from that of Victoria Pendencia, he had just been told the price he was going to have to pay for the guns he needed.

"Can't you do better than that?" he asked the seller's representative.

"I am sorry, *señor*," the man said, "but you will do no better anywhere else for price or quality."

Benito frowned, but knew he had no choice.

"Where will they be delivered."

"On the beach, by Jalapa."

Jalapa was a small town directly east of Mexico City, near the Gulf of Mexico.

"When?"

"Three days, just before dusk."

"Very well."

The seller's representative looked at Victoria and Benito, who were the only two people in the room besides himself. Manuel was keeping watch outside. The representative said, "Until then."

As the man started for the door, Benito called out his name, "Paco."

"Sí, Benito?"

"You should be in this with us."

"I am in this for myself, Benito," Paco said, and then added, "like everyone else."

He left and Victoria said, "What did he mean?"

"He is cynical." Benito picked up his hat and said, "I must return to camp."

"Not yet, Benito—"

"Victoria," Benito said, regarding her fondly, "I must return to Delores—"

"No, it's not that, Benito," she said to the man she had once thought she loved. Now, since meeting Clint Adams, she was not sure anymore. "There is someone I wish you to meet."

"A man?" he asked, looking amused.

"I have recruited him."

The amused look vanished and was replaced by one of stone.

"You have no authority—"

"When you hear his name," she said, "you will not be angry."

"What is it, then?"

"Clint Adams."

"Adams," Benito said, finding the name familiar but momentarily unable to place it. His mind was on other things—like Delores.

"In America they call him the Gunsmith."

"The Gunsmith!" Benito said. He thought a moment and then said, "I suppose such a man could be of help to us, but . . ."

"But what, Benito?" Victoria asked, frowning. His

reaction was not at all what she had expected—but then her reactions of late were not what she would have expected, either, especially when it came to Clint.

"With this man, this ghost that *I* have recruited, I fear hiring another like him."

"Clint is not like him," Victoria said, perhaps a bit too forcefully.

"How do you know this?"

"I have . . . come to know him."

Benito frowned. He had always found Victoria's obvious affection for him flattering . . . and tempting. Was he feeling a twinge of jealousy now?

"All right, Victoria," he said, putting his hand on her shoulder, "I will meet this man that you have come to know so well."

"Gracias, Benito."

"Take me to him."

"It is early—"

"Now!"

"*Sí*, Benito."

She led the way out of the building and along the darkening streets of Mexico City, hoping that Clint would not mind if they showed up early.

She was mildly shocked to find that she was more worried abut what Clint thought than what Benito, her leader, did.

TWENTY-ONE

When the knock came on Clint's door, he frowned. It was too early for Victoria to be showing up, with or without her Benito, but . . .

He opened the door and when he saw the two of them standing there he was not surprised.

Benito was a very tall, broad Mexican who looked naked without crisscrossing bandoleers on his chest. He appeared to be in his late thirties, unshaven, and badly in need of a bath. He did not look like a man who would fit easily into the President's Palace. He *looked* like a bandit leader and not a rebel leader.

And there was another problem. Even before the two men spoke one word to each other, Clint knew that they would not like each other. There was a lot of tension in the air and he wasn't sure what it came from. Maybe the man didn't like gringos, or maybe it had something to do with Victoria. Whatever it was, Clint was going to have to try to get past it.

"Victoria."

"Clint, we are early," she said, apologetically. "I hope you don't—"

"Do not apologize to the gringo, Victoria," Benito said, interrupting her.

"Don't worry about it, Victoria," Clint said, ignoring the big man. He put his hand on her shoulder to assure her that it was all right, and she smiled at him warily. Benito, on the other hand, glared at him.

"Come in," he invited, stepping back.

Victoria entered readily, Benito with some trepidation, as if he were expecting a trap. Clint thought it would be better to talk here than in the hotel's dining room, where Benito would be sure to attract attention.

He said as much, and Benito simply grunted.

"Victoria tells me you wish to work for us," Benito said, "for the revolution."

"Victoria's mistaken."

Benito's eyebrows went up in surprise, as did Victoria's. She gave Clint a puzzled look.

"Victoria came to me," Clint told the rebel leader, "with her friend Manuel, who I'm sure is outside in a doorway, someplace."

The fact of the matter was that Manuel was standing across the street in a corner doorway at that very moment—the only doorway Clint was able to see from his window.

"I'm sorry I can't offer you much in the way of accommodations," Clint said. Indicating the room's only chair he said to Benito, "You can sit there. Victoria, why don't you sit on the bed?"

Victoria started for the bed but Benito's voice stopped her.

"There is no need for us to sit," Benito said. "We will not be staying that long."

"All right, fine," Clint said, "we'll remain standing. Benito, I understand you want to start a revolution."

"The revolution has started," Benito replied, his back stiffening.

"Really? I haven't heard anything about it."

"It has started in the minds of the people," Benito said, puffing out his chest. "As soon as we have the guns that we need, we will be able to give the people what they want."

"And what is that?"

"A government that will care for them."

"That's a nobel aim," Clint said, "but you'll need help to get there."

"From you?"

"From anyone you can get. I've never known a revolution that cared much about the means it took to gain its end," Clint remarked.

Benito frowned, and Clint thought the man might be having trouble following his English.

"All right," Clint said, "I want to help, but I won't do it for free."

"Of course not."

"Even you, Benito, must admit that you will come out of this with a profit—if it is successful. That is all I'm asking for myself. That doesn't sound so unreasonable, does it?" Clint asked.

"All right," Benito said after a moment. "You are an Americano legend, and we will pay you that way."

"Fine. How?"

"That does not matter," Benito said. "You and your kind simply wish to be paid, and you will be."

"Have you hired many of my kind, as you put it?" Clint asked, hoping to draw out something about what other mercenaries they had hired—like Hickok's ghost.

"Enough," Benito said, and then thinking of the man James Butler added, "more than enough."

"Okay, then I'm hired," Clint said. He approached Benito and extended his hand, but Benito ignored it and made for the door.

"I will notify you when you are needed," Benito said, "and I expect you to obey without question."

"As long as I get paid."

"I will contact you through Victoria." He looked at Victoria then and said, "Are you coming?"

"You are returning to camp?"

"*Sí.*"

Then I will stay here . . . for a while," she said, somewhat timidly.

Benito hesitated, then opened the door and left, banging it shut behind him. Victoria remained seated on the bed, her hands folded in her lap.

Clint looked at Victoria and said, "So that's your leader, huh?"

She looked at him, smiled sadly, and said, "He was the only man with enough courage to *be* leader."

Benito had not greatly impressed Clint and he was glad that he was not really signing up for this revolution.

He didn't have high hopes for its success.

TWENTY-TWO

After Benito left, they made love and then Clint suggested they go downstairs and have dinner.

"You'll stay the night with me?" he asked.

"Yes," she answered without hesitation.

"Good."

Over dinner he asked her to tell her something about Benito.

"I know Benito . . . and yet I don't," she said. "I met him when I joined the revolution."

"Who got you involved?"

"Manuel. He is . . . in love with me, as you said."

"And you? Who are you in love with?"

"I thought I was in love with Benito," she said. "I was impressed by his desire to help the people and by his leadership . . ."

"And now?"

"Now I do not know," she said. "Now I am . . . confused."

"Because of me?"

She nodded.

"I'm sorry, Victoria," he said. "I didn't come here

to confuse you, or make you doubt your revolution, or your leader, but the simple fact is that I was not impressed by Benito. Maybe he's not at his best in a hotel room, though. I'm willing to give him the benefit of the doubt and wait to see him in action.''

"I, too," she said, "am waiting to see him in action. I am waiting to see any kind of action.''

"Benito said he needed guns.''

"He is getting them.''

"Where?''

"I don't know. I have heard that there is a man who sells guns who was once with Maximilian, but I do not know if this is where he is getting our guns.''

Braxton!—Clint thought.

Benito was buying his guns from Jonathan Braxton. Of course, Braxton had even mentioned to Clint that he had a big deal coming up and that he didn't care who won the revolution.

"All right," he said to her, "now I know who he's getting the guns from.''

"Is that why you are here?'' she asked, suddenly looking alarmed. "Are you working with the federales?''

"No, no," he said, quickly taking her hands to allay her suspicions.

"Then why?'' she asked. "You are not here for the revolution. You are not that kind of man.''

He stared at her for a few seconds, then decided to confide in her.

"All right, Victoria, I'll tell you why I'm here.''

She ignored her food after that and gave him her full attention.

"I'm looking for a man, a friend of mine who is supposed to be dead.''

"Then how can you be looking for him?"

He explained to her about the rumors that said that Wild Bill Hickok was alive and in Mexico, and he was seeking to find out the basis for these rumors.

"I don't really expect to find my friend alive," he added, "but if someone is using his name, I want to make sure he stops."

Victoria had a funny look on her face then and Clint asked her what was wrong.

"Something that Benito said today after I told him about you."

"What did he say?"

"That he had hired a ghost."

"Then I'm right!" Clint said with feeling. "Whether it's Hickok or not, the man has become involved in the revolution."

He reached across the table to grasp her hands again and said, "Victoria, I must find this man."

"Then you have no intentions of helping us with the revolution?" she inquired.

When she asked that, he thought that perhaps he'd misread her feelings about him and about the revolution. If she were still devoted to overthrowing Díaz, then he'd put his foot in it because she would give him up to Benito the first chance she got.

"Victoria, I'm sorry," he said, "but you were right. This is not my country, and I am not a mercenary. I don't hire out my gun, no matter what my reputation might lead people to think."

She remained silent.

"On the other hand, I am not here to hinder your revolution in any way. If you go through with it, I wish you only the best of luck."

"If we go through with it?"

"I haven't seen much of it, not beyond you and Manuel and Benito, but I can't honestly say I expect it to succeed. I may be wrong. I don't know how many men Benito has."

"Not many," she admitted.

"Then how can he have a revolution."

"Benito's plan is to get enough guns and weapons to storm the palace and take Díaz out and shoot him in front of the people."

"That's his plan?" Clint asked, incredulous. "Victoria, that's . . . that's *bandit* thinking. He's planning to loot the palace."

She shrugged and said, "Benito is, after all, a bandit. How else would he think?"

Clint decided there and then to do what he could to keep Victoria from taking part in the revolution, but first he had to find his ghost.

"Victoria, will you try to help me?"

He studied her face while she thought, and he could see that there was considerable turmoil going on inside her head. She was trying to examine the conflict of interest in helping him, and he could only hope that she would decide in his favor.

"All right, Clint," she said finally, "I will help you—as long as it does not hurt the revolution."

"Fine," he said, "agreed. Thank you."

"Perhaps we should finish our dinner?" she asked. "Then we can go back upstairs."

"Yes," Clint said, "perhaps we should."

They spent the night together and the following morning Victoria left him, promising to try to find out about his friend for him.

"Don't forget," Clint reminded her, watching with pleasure as she dressed.

"What?"

"If you locate the man, I don't want him to know I'm here."

"I can't help it if Benito tells him," she said, slipping into her shirt, hiding her breasts from him. Up to that point he had been watching them grow taut, rise and fall with her every move.

"Benito," Clint said, rising and taking her by the shoulders, "won't tell anyone anything more than he thinks that person should know."

"All right," she said, "I'll be careful of what I say."

"That's my girl," he said, kissing her. "Thanks for helping me, Victoria."

"*De nada*," she said softly and left.

After she was gone, Clint dressed and did some thinking. He wondered if perhaps he should have come to Mexico City under some assumed name to join the revolution. That way there would have been no danger of the man who assumed Hickok's name recognizing his—unless he knew him by sight. However, without his reputation as the Gunsmith, there would have been no guarantee that he *would* have been accepted by the revolution.

He walked to the window to look down at the side street and the sliver of the front street that he was allowed a view of. He spotted Manuel, either still standing in the doorway, or once again taking up position there. Either way it looked as if Benito still wanted him watched—or perhaps Manuel was watching Victoria.

He stood by the window awhile longer until he was sure Victoria'd had time to leave the hotel, and Manuel was also still there, so he was certain that the man was watching him.

Let him stand there, then. Clint decided to go downstairs and eat breakfast in the hotel dining room and he hoped that Manuel hadn't eaten yet.

TWENTY-THREE

While Benito was making his way back to the rebel camp, the man he knew as James Butler was doing some thinking. By his count, there were about forty men in this camp. He had no way of knowing if there were more somewhere else—and if there weren't, they were all fools—but he knew one thing. If, when the time came for him to make his play for the war chest, they were out in the open, he was going to have a hell of a time taking it away from forty men.

The thing to do was to cut the odds, so he left Delores on the pallet in the cave and went out to talk to some of the men. With a little luck—and some help from human nature—by the time Benito got back, he should have been able to sway a few of the men over to his side, enough so that, with the element of surprise on their side, they'd be able to hold off the rest and make off with the revolution's war chest, but not too many that he wouldn't be able to kill them all after they'd gotten away with it.

The first man he talked to was Chico, and he was immediately encouraged.

With the promise of a fortune to split among them, a half a dozen men in all were able to be brought over to his way of thinking.

Just enough.

Jonathan Braxton was very pleased.

Paco had returned from Mexico City with the news that the deal had been struck with the rebel leader, Benito. Braxton himself knew that all the weapons and ammunition he was selling to the rebels wasn't going to do them much good. For one thing, their leadership was suspect, and for another their forces were too small, too untrained, and poorly motivated.

Fortunately, Benito had been able to raise enough money for the deal—but beyond that, he had very little.

For all of these reasons—taken singly or collectively—many revolutions had failed.

This one, he felt sure, would be no different.

However, in all revolutions, there is someone who profits, and this one would be no different in that respect, either.

Jonathan Braxton would profit, and he'd be ready to profit from the next one as well.

"Papa," Carlotta called softly, breaking into Braxton's thoughts. He turned, smiled at her, and invited her into his office to join him.

"When the ship comes, Papa, will you be going also?"

"No, my dear," Braxton said, "Paco will be going to oversee the transaction. Why?"

"I was hoping to go with you, and then—"

"And then to Mexico City? Hoping to see Clint Adams?"

She smiled shyly and looked at the floor.

"My dear, once this cargo is delivered, Mexico City will be no place for people like us. Not for some time . . . not until the turmoil subsides."

"But I've never been to Mexico City, Papa," she complained.

"You will, darling," he said, putting his arm around her. "When the French come, when it is civilized again, you will."

"When will that be?" she asked, hopefully.

"Soon," he lied, "very soon, Carlotta."

When Benito reached camp, he entered his headquarters immediately and found Delores inside sitting stiffly.

"Delores?" he said.

"That animal," she said, "that brute. The day must come soon when I can kill him, Benito," she said bitterly. "It must be soon!"

"It will be soon," he said, not touching her.

Lately, he couldn't bring himself to touch her. He wondered if when the revolution was all over and he was *El Presidente* if he shouldn't take another woman—another wife—as his First Lady, someone who had not given up her virtue for the cause. He appreciated her sacrifice, of course, but he didn't think she would make the ideal President's wife. On top of everything else, she was beginning to look older.

Someone like Victoria, perhaps, would better fulfill that position. Young, beautiful . . . of course, if she had submitted to Clint Adams . . .

"Benito," Delores said, interrupting his thoughts, "is there something wrong?"

"No," he said, abruptly. "The bargain has been made for the guns. We are to pick them up in three days at the beach by Jalapa."

She seemed uncomfortable for some reason, as if her clothes were irritating her.

She came close to him and he imagined that he could smell the gringo on her. He tried not to draw away from her.

"I do not trust the gringo," she said.

"What did he say?"

"He was asking about money."

Benito laughed harshly and said, "The mercenaries care for very little else. I have hired another American legend who will lend his name to our cause and perhaps his gun."

"Another like Butler?" she asked, the distaste plain on her face.

"Not quite like Butler," Benito said, and then thinking of Victoria he said, "but his fate will be exactly the same."

Victoria was thinking about Clint Adams. What was it about the man that made her forget everything else— even the revolution, which she had thought was important to her—when she was with him, or when she was thinking about him?

She was in her room, trying to figure out a way to find out what Clint wanted to know, if his friend—this Hickok he had told her about during the night—was the other gringo mercenary that Benito called a ghost. Would Manuel know? Perhaps.

He was, after all, Benito's brother.

● ● ●

Manuel stood in his doorway, fuming angrily.

He was the next Mexican President's brother, and yet he was given menial tasks to perform. He didn't mind having to stay with Victoria, but following the gringo around, that was a job anyone could do.

Benito thought he was weak, he thought, and then grinning tightly to himself he added that he would show his older brother that he was not. He would show his brother that he was as strong and capable as the next Presidente of Mexico.

Manuel loved Victoria—even more, he thought, than the revolution—and he had seen her leave the hotel early that morning. That meant that she had spent the night with the gringo, in his bed.

For that, the gringo legend would die, and then what would his brother think of him after he had single-handedly killed the Gunsmith?

TWENTY-FOUR

When Clint left the hotel, he felt Manuel dogging his trail. He thought that the man was probably just doing his duty, following him, so it never occurred to him that he might have something else on his mind.

The Gunsmith really had no specific destination in mind. He was simply walking, heading in the direction of the President's Palace. Maybe he'd take a look with a critical eye and judge what kind of chance heavily armed men would have of successfully storming the place. He'd asked Victoria during the night how many men Benito had, but she didn't know the answer. The most she had ever seen at one time, she'd said, was forty. He'd keep at least that number in mind.

He got lost.

He must have taken a wrong turn somewhere, but instead of turning back he went on, seeing a part of the city he hadn't seen before. It seemed to be a cross between the more affluent section of the city and the part that Victoria had taken him to, where she lived.

Steering by some sort of instinct, he abandoned the main streets and decided to take an alley that looked as if it cut straight through to another street. He was still aware of Victoria's would-be suitor, Manuel, on his trail, but suddenly the man seemed to have closed the gap between them, as if he were trying to get closer for some reason.

If he were simply tailing the Gunsmith to see where he came and went, there would have been no reason for him to get closer.

Clint suddenly felt a chill on the back of his neck.

When the Gunsmith turned down the alley, Manuel saw his chance. He knew the alley was fairly long, and he hurried to close the gap between them. He removed the old Navy Colt from his belt and held it tightly in his hand.

He had never fired it before.

Clint heard the sound of the hammer on a gun being cocked, and reacted by reflex. There was only one reason for that sound to be heard behind a man's back, so he simply whirled, drew, and fired.

His bullet caught a stunned Manuel in the chest, punching right through and out the back. His finger yanked convulsively on the trigger of the Colt, which fired into the ground. The man swayed and was dead before he fell to the ground.

Clint walked to the fallen man to check him and found him dead. He started to wonder what had prompted the man to try to kill him, and then it dawned on him. He had undoubtedly seen Victoria leave the hotel that morning and knew that they'd spent the night together. That was enough reason for any man to kill.

He was holstering his gun, standing over the dead man, when the men suddenly arrived.

TWENTY-FIVE

"You must understand, Señor Adams," Lieutenant Cesar Valdez said. "We cannot allow our citizens to be shot down in the streets. Our President, Porfirio Díaz, fought for law and order."

"I understand."

Clint was seated in the lieutenant's office in the headquarters.

"Now, you are fortunate that the man you killed was a known—how shall I put it?—undesirable."

"I see."

"And there are no witnesses to dispute your story."

"I see," Clint said again.

The lieutenant was a man of modest height, which was probably the reason he was standing while he had invited—rather strongly—the Gunsmith to be seated. The man was spotless. His nails were clean, his hair was neatly cut and combed, his uniform was without blemish, and his boots gleamed. He carried a riding crop, which he had a habit of striking against his right leg as he spoke.

"Therefore, I believe that it will be possible for us to allow you to go free—"

"Good," Clint interjected quickly.

"—with but a small fine."

"A fine? For shooting an 'undesirable'?"

The man looked at him in surprise and said, "For disturbing the peace, *señor*."

"Of course."

"Once you have paid the fine, we will return your weapon to you."

Clint asked what the fine was and paid it without complaint, even though it was high. Still, he was able to pay it without using all of his money, so he did.

"May I have my gun now?"

"Of course."

The man walked around behind his desk and took the Gunsmith's modified Colt out of his top drawer, but instead of handing it over, he studied it, frowning.

"Señor Adams," he said very seriously, "you are a very famous man, even here in Mexico."

"I'm flattered."

"Please do not be," Valdez said. "I am not impressed; I am merely stating a fact. My point is this. Should certain—uh—factions here in my country learn of your presence, they might be tempted to—uh—recruit your services."

"My services, Lieutenant, are not for sale."

"Ah, I am very happy to hear that, *señor*," Valdez said, handing Clint his gun across his desk. "Please do your best to keep it that way, eh?"

"I'll try."

"And one other thing, *señor*," the lieutenant said as Clint walked to the door.

"Yes?" Clint asked.

The lieutenant fixed him with what he was sure was supposed to be a menacing look and said, "Please try not to kill anyone else while you are in my city. It would not be advisable."

"I'll try my best."

"And if you must," Valdez added, "make it a gringo, and not a Mexican citizen, eh?"

Clint had offered no resistance whatsoever to the two soldiers who had found him standing over Manuel's body. He had willingly surrendered his gun and allowed himself to be escorted to the garrison for questioning.

Valdez had kept him waitng for two hours and then questioned him for the better part of a third.

Who was he? What was he doing in Mexico? Why did he kill a Mexican citizen?

Clint felt all along that they would probably release him and were simply making him sweat it out.

Now that he was free, he had to find Victoria. He hoped to explain to her satisfaction what had happened with Manuel, and he fervently hoped that this incident would not hurt his chance of finding the man he was seeking among the rebel forces.

He hoped that Manuel would not turn out to be somebody important. After an hour he gave up trying to find Victoria's room and decided to go back to his hotel and simply wait for her there.

He just hoped that she wouldn't somehow hear about it before he got a chance to explain.

TWENTY-SIX

He was considering going downstairs for dinner when there was a knock at the door. It was Victoria.

"Hello," she said, smiling, and he knew she hadn't heard anything.

"Come on in."

She entered shyly and turned to face him as she shut the door. "I wasn't able to find out anything," she said apologetically. "I think we will have to wait for Benito to come back—unless I can find out something from Manuel."

"Victoria—"

"I don't understand why I haven't been able to find him today," she went on with a puzzled look.

She walked to his window and looked out, trying to make it seem casual.

"He's not there."

"What?" she asked, turning to face him.

"He's not across the street, Victoria."

"Who?"

"Manuel. Come on, I know he's been watching me, either for you or Benito."

"I, uh—"

"Victoria, I have to tell you something," he said, taking her hands in his.

"What?"

"How close are you to Manuel?"

She shrugged. "We are friends."

"He loves you."

"Yes."

"But you don't love him?"

"No. What is it, Clint? What's wrong?"

"When I left the hotel this morning, Manuel followed me, as he was supposed to do."

"And?"

"Then he did something I don't think he was supposed to do."

"What?"

"He tried to kill me."

"You must be mistaken," Victoria said.

"He tried to shoot me in the back."

She opened her mouth, either to ask him if he was all right, or if Manuel was all right, but then she shut it quickly and stared a moment before saying, "And you killed him."

"If I hadn't," he said, squeezing her hands, "I wouldn't be here, Victoria."

She looked into his eyes and said, "I understand that."

"Well, I just want you to know I am sorry," he said. "I hope it doesn't make things harder . . . with Benito."

"It might," she said.

"Why? Was Manuel somebody important to the revolution?"

"Perhaps not," Victoria said, "but he was somebody important to Benito."

Clint frowned and said, "I don't understand."

"Manuel was Benito's brother," she responded. Clint stared at her for a few seconds and then said, "That's fine."

Proving that she had a brain as well as beauty, Victoria said, "It may not be as bad as you think."

"Why?"

"Who knows that you killed Manuel?"

"You and I . . . and Lieutenant Valdez."

She arched an eyebrow at him and said, "You and I aren't going to tell him."

He caught on.

"And Benito certainly won't go to the garrison to find out."

She nodded.

"Victoria—"

"Lying about Manuel will not hurt the revolution, Clint," she said, explaining why she was doing it. "In fact, he might be so consumed with a desire for revenge against you that he would neglect the revolution. This way he will concentrate and when he is President he will use that position to try to find out who killed Manuel." She gave him a long look then and said, "By that time you will be gone, won't you?"

"Hopefully," he said.

"But not for a little while at least?"

"No," he said, enclosing her in his arms, "not for a little while."

In bed later Clint asked Victoria a question she balked at answering.

"When are they picking up their guns?"

"Clint—"

"I could have asked you where as well, Victoria."

"I can't—"

"All right," Clint said, "I shouldn't have asked. I'm compromising you enough as it is."

Clint was almost sure that Victoria would have been present at any discussion concerning the guns. She was apparently Benito's Mexico City contact and would have arranged the meetings between Benito and Braxton's representative, probably his man Paco.

"Clint, I believe that you are not here to stop the revolution. I want to help you . . ."

"Shh," he said, holding her tightly. "I don't want you to tell me anything you don't want to."

"If I can find out about your friend—or this man who claims to be Hickok—and I find out that he will be present when the weapons are delivered, then I will tell you where that is—if Benito doesn't."

"You think Benito will?"

"If he is going to use you," she said, "he will want you to be there at the exchange to make sure it goes well."

"All right," he said. "I can accept that. All I want is to see this man who is claiming to be Hickok."

"I promise you that I will do my best to see that happens."

With that, Clint felt reasonably certain that he would be seeing Hickok, the ghost of Hickok, or the Hickok imposter within the next few days.

TWENTY-SEVEN

James Butler had his six men lined up and was only waiting for Benito to name the time and place when they would be picking up the revolution's war chest. He was hoping to grab it before they got to the point where the exchange of payment and guns was to take place.

He had Chico even more firmly on his side in that the Mexican had agreed to help him kill the other five men once they had the war chest firmly in hand and removed to a point where they were supposed to split it.

Once that was done and there were only the two of them left, it would be a showdown between them, and Butler was certain he'd have no problem doing away with Chico. He had no idea what was in Chico's mind, but he'd be watching the man very carefully.

However, he was destined to be disappointed because when he awoke the morning before the exchange was to be made, he saw that Benito and one other man were gone from camp.

"Where is Benito?" he demanded of Delores.

"He left camp early."

"For what?"

She glared at him and he smiled at her, knowing that she hated him and would gladly kill him the first chance she got—once they didn't need him anymore.

"He went to get the money, didn't he?" he said, suddenly realizing that this was what he would have done. "Benito doesn't trust any of his men, does he?"

"He trusts as many as necessary," she said. "We will meet him where the exchange is to be made for the guns."

"You know where that is?"

"We will meet him there," she said again, firmly.

Butler thought he might be able to force her to tell him where that was, but there were too many men in camp for him to handle if she decided to cry out.

"All right," he said, backing away. "If that's the way you want it."

He went in search of Benito because now he knew they were going to have to be prepared to take the money—and whatever else made up the war chest—by force from the full complement of men who were in this camp—and who knew how many men would be making the delivery?

It didn't matter, though, how many men he had to take it from. The war chest had to have a sizable total to finance a revolution, and he was going to get it—no matter how many lives it cost.

Other people's lives.

Benito had gone to get the war chest alone. He had taken the extra man with him to send into Mexico City to tell Manuel and Victoria to meet him and the other men at the exchange sight on the beach by Jalapa.

Included in his message was that they should bring the Gunsmith with them.

"I want a man to watch him at all times," Valdez was telling his men, the five of them who were lined up in front of his desk.

He was speaking about Clint Adams, the Gunsmith.

"Lieutenant," one of the men spoke up, "forgive me, but what makes one gringo so important?"

"*This* gringo," Valdez said, "is not a normal man; he is a legend, and this is a legend who is alive, not a ghost. I am more concerned with this gringo than with the rumors about the other one, the man called Wild Bill. Besides," he added wryly, "this one we can follow. A ghost we cannot even find. That's all. As soon as it looks like he is going to leave town, I want to know about it."

The men saluted and left to work out among themselves the sequence they would follow in watching the man.

Cesar Valdez sat back in his chair with a satisfied sigh. The rebels would not be able to resist recruiting a man like the Gunsmith. When they did—or even *after* they did—he would be there to gather them all up. It would be a considerable feather in his cap when he cleaned out the rebels and let Presidente Díaz know that it was all his doing.

And he would *definitely* make sure *El Presidente* knew.

Thanks to the rebels, to the Gunsmith, and to the rumors of a ghost, a promotion was looming in Valdez's near future.

● ● ●

"The ship will be here this evening," Braxton told Paco. "I will go onboard only to inspect the cargo and make sure it is as is it supposed to be. You will then stay onboard and accompany it to the beach at Jalapa."

"*Sí, padrino*," Paco said.

"Be on the alert for any sign of betrayal," Braxton said. "Your men will meet you there, right?"

"*Sí, padrino*. They have their instructions and will be at the beach before the ship."

"Many of the rebels will be there as well. What is your impression of Benito?"

Paco made a face. "He is wasting a lot of money, *padrino*, but I believe that he is sincere."

Shaking his head, Braxton said, "It would take a lot more than sincerity to overthrow Díaz—and someone who is more than a mountain bandit to engineer it."

"*Es verdad*," Paco said, agreeing.

"All right, Paco. Get some rest tonight. You will need to be alert."

"Good night, *padrino*."

There was a time Paco had been deathly afraid of ships and water, but after a few deliveries he had come to accept that he had to be the *padrino*'s representative onboard, the one who made sure that the weapons got to where they were supposed to go. Paco was the man who oversaw the delivery of the guns, paid the captain of the ship, and accepted payment from the customer— in this case, Benito.

However, he was still deathly afraid of the water.

Braxton poured himself one last brandy before retiring for the night, and he thought about Clint Adams.

He hoped that the famous Gunsmith would decide to

take him up on his offer of a partnership. Now that it had been some time since he made the offer he could think of several arguments he could have used to persuade the man, but the one that came most readily to mind was the fact that it would allow the Gunsmith to settle down. Surely a man who has faced death for most of his life must tire of it eventually.

Hopefully, Clint Adams would see it that way and would agree not only to become Braxton's partner—but he also hoped that he would marry Carlotta for he could think of no better choice for a son-in-law.

A man could dream—but it was also up to a man to make his dream come true.

TWENTY-EIGHT

The man Benito sent to town was named Carlos Sierra. The first place he went to find Victoria was her room. When he found she was not there, he followed Benito's instructions and went to the gringo's hotel. Benito did not seem happy when he suggested this, and this puzzled Carlos. After all, Benito was married to Delores, not Victoria. Why should he mind if she slept with the gringo Adams? What really puzzled Carlos was how Benito could allow Delores to lie with the gringo, James Butler.

Carlos was a young man in his early twenties without much experience with women. They were an enigma to him, and the actions of Delores and Victoria did nothing to make them clearer to him.

Carlos asked the clerk for the gringo's room number, and he went upstairs wondering if he would indeed find Victoria there with him.

He did.

"This is Carlos," Victoria said.

Luckily, they had been in the act of getting dressed when he knocked on the door.

Clint had answered the door and the young Mexican had asked him if he was Señor Adams. At that point, Victoria joined Clint at the door and made the introduction.

"Did Benito send you?" she asked him.

"*Sí*, to find you and Manuel."

Clint felt Victoria freeze for a second, but she covered up well.

"Manuel is not here, Carlos. What does Benito want?"

"We will be picking up the guns tomorrow," Carlos said. He looked at Clint warily and added, "You know where."

"Yes, I do."

"Benito wants you and Manuel to come and bring Señor Adams."

"All right."

Carlos stood there awkwardly for a moment, not realizing that it was time for him to leave.

"What are you to do after you give us the message?"

"Return to camp."

"Then do so," she said. "We will be there tomorrow."

"*Sí*," Carlos said, and he finally turned and left.

Clint closed the door and turned to face Victoria.

"Where will we be meeting?" he asked.

She hesitated only a moment and then said, "The Gulf. On the beach near a town called Jalapa."

"The guns are coming in by ship?"

"Yes."

"From Braxton."

"Who?"

"The man who once worked for Maximilian."

"Is that his name?"

"Yes."

"How do you know?"

"I met him a short time ago on my way here."

She looked suspicious for a moment, but he said, "I didn't know at the time that he was involved with the revolution."

"I believe you."

"Let's go downstairs and get some breakfast."

"What will you do?" she asked. "When you find who you're looking for, I mean."

"That depends," he said. "If I find the man and he is Hickok I'll give him a hug, and then give him hell for letting me think he was dead."

"And if it isn't Hickok?"

"That depends, too. If it's someone who is trying to cash in on his name and reputation, I'll make him sorry the idea ever occurred to him."

"You'll kill him?"

"I've killed a lot of men in my life, Victoria," Clint said, "but I don't think I ever intended ahead of time to kill very many of them."

"That means you don't know."

"That means that I don't plan to," he said. "There's another possibility in there also."

"What?"

"That the man might actually be Wild Bill Hickok's ghost."

"Do you really believe that?" she asked, gaping at him. "Do you believe in ghosts?"

He'd forgotten how superstitious the Mexican people were.

"I never have," Clint said, "but the simple fact that I'm here because of a rumor indicates that I must believe in them, even if it's just a little."

He reached for the door knob and said again, "Let's go and get some breakfast."

"There is something I must tell you," she said, hurriedly grabbing his arm and holding it tightly.

"What?"

She hesitated now, unsure of whether or not she should go on.

"Victoria—"

"Wait," she told him, and he could see that she was wrestling with herself. He took his hand off the door knob, fearing that leaving it there might rush her.

"I think—" she started, then stopped, composed herself, and said, "I am in love with you."

He had known that was coming somehow, and it didn't sound so bad—although he was not prepared to repeat the words to her. Not yet, anyway.

"Victoria—"

She stopped him by placing her fingertips against his mouth, silently telling him that there was either no need for him to reply, or that *she* didn't want to discuss it right then.

"Let's go downstairs and have some breakfast," she said instead.

Breakfast—and the remainder of the day, for that matter—was strained.

Clint was sure that he could guess some of the thoughts that were going through her mind.

Was she being unfaithful to the revolution by helping him, even by loving him—and he would have accepted that statement more had she made it the way she originally began to—that she *thought* she was in love with. She had changed her mind and made the statement without reservation—but how could she be so sure in such a short period of time.

Then again, how had he been so sure so quickly that time ago when he had loved Joanna Morgan?

Sometimes you just know.

Granting that she loved him, she would have been thinking about whether she was being unfaithful to him by telling him everything he wanted to know right away?

He had no intention of making her choose between him and the revolution. *He* didn't actually feel that he was forcing her to do anything that was against the revolution. He certainly never had intentions of hindering any chance for success that it might have.

He hoped that she'd keep her convictions and not hold it against him if the revolution failed.

Benito had left a buckboard at the place where he'd hidden the war chest and now he had finished loading onto it the money and other things that made up the revolution's treasury.

Some of it was very heavy, especially the gold candle holder he had stolen from a church. He was not ashamed of that because he had known he was doing it for the cause. There were other items of gold and silver that he knew would be melted down by the gunrunners, but it was only the candle holder that he thought about. Maybe he'd be able to leave it behind . . . but no. It would take all that they had to pay for the guns, and ideally they should have even more weapons than they were getting, but Benito couldn't wait.

He unsaddled his horse, tossed the saddle onto the back of the buckboard, and then hooked his horse up to the buckboard. Two horses would have been better, but they were not so very far from the beach. He had known the place that would be used, so he had hidden the money, gold, and silver nearby.

He built a fire to cook and for warmth, and he sat by it, drinking coffee and hoping that all would go as planned tomorrow. If it did, then by the end of the week—with some luck—he would be in the President's Palace, with his brother Manuel as his Vice President, and Victoria as his First Lady.

Nothing would go wrong; he could feel it! He even knew that the two gringos—Butler, who claimed to be Wild Bill Hickok, and Clint Adams, who *was* the Gunsmith—would both die a far finer death than either man deserved.

They would be dying so that Mexico could live.

Lt. Valdez listened intently as his sergeant reported to him on the latest movements of Clint Adams and the girl, his hands lingering over his cooling dinner.

"And just before dinner," the soldier said, "they went to the livery stable to check on Señor Adams's horse. After that they—"

"To check on his horse?" Valdez said, stopping the man mid-sentence.

"And what about the woman? Does she own a horse?"

"I do not know."

"Well, find out, man!"

"*Sí, Comandante.*"

"And what would that indicate to you, Sergeant, that the gringo was checking on his horse?"

"I do not know."

"Stupid," Valdez said, but not with any heat. He

said it tiredly. "It means the gringo wanted to be sure
that his horse would be ready to ride tomorrow."

"In the morning?"

"I don't know when," Valdez snapped, "I just know
that I want two men watching his hotel tonight and tomorrow. If he leaves town, one will follow and the
other will report to me. Understood?"

"*Sí, Comandante.*"

Something was going to happen tomorrow, Valdez
thought, now ignoring his cold dinner.

He could feel it!

Tomorrow he would take one giant step toward his
promotion.

"Victoria?" Clint said during the night.

"Clint, you do not have to say—"

"Quiet," he said. "This is business. Did you see the
soldiers who were following us today?"

"Soldiers? Following us?"

"They switched off during the course of the day, but
there was always one behind us. There are two outside
the hotel now."

"But how could you—"

"I have a sixth sense about being followed or
watched," he said.

"But if they follow us tomorrow—"

"They don't know that they've been spotted, which
is in our favor," he explained.

"What will we do?"

"We'll figure something out," he said, "by morning. Go to sleep, now."

She went to sleep, and he laid awake, figuring something out and coming to a decision well before morning.

● ● ●

James Butler decided that he was tired of waiting.

He got hold of Chico and told him to get the rest of the men who were with them. After that, he told them to take up positions in front of the headquarters cave, and he went inside to talk to Delores.

"What do you want?" she demanded. She was standing at the heavy wooden table that Benito used for making his plans—although Butler had little regard for any plans Benito might have made.

"It's time," he said, moving toward her.

"For what?" she demanded. "I am finished playing your whore, gringo—"

When he reached her, he struck her a vicious backhand across the face, knocking her to the cave floor. Pointing at her with his right index finger, he said, "It's time to stop playing game. I want to know where Benito is, where the war chest is, and where the site for the exchange is—and think before you answer, Delores, my sweet. Every answer you give me that I don't like will cause you a lot of pain."

TWENTY-NINE

When Clint awoke in the morning, he went out to make his arrangements. As he returned to the room, he saw that Victoria was awake. She had a puzzled look on her face, but as he walked in, it vanished.

"I was wondering where you were?"

"I had to go out and make some arrangements."

"What kind of arrangements?" she asked, sitting up and wiping the sleep from her eyes.

He sat on the bed with her and said, "The horses are outside."

"But it's early."

"That's all right; I want to get there early. I want to look the place over."

"What—what about the soldiers?"

"We don't have to worry about them," he said. "I've taken care of them."

"How?"

He smiled and said, "Money takes care of a lot of things, Victoria." He pulled the sheet off her so that she was totally nude. "Come on now; get dressed."

She gave him a coy look and said, "Do you really want me to . . . now?"

He grinned back, reached for her, and said, "I guess not."

It was still early morning when they got downstairs for breakfast, and they ate in thoughtful silence. Clint thought of talking to her just to keep her mind off what she was doing, but that wouldn't have been right. He was giving her every opportunity to change her mind about helping him, but somehow he didn't think she would. Still, she deserved the chance.

After breakfast they stood up and looked at each other across the table.

"Ready?" he asked her.

She gave him a short nod and said, "Ready."

They went outside to the horses, and he could see her looking around for the soldiers.

He hoped she wouldn't spot any.

"Victoria, how long a ride will this be?"

"A few hours at least," she said. "We will ride through Jalapa to the beach."

"Well, I'm bringing along some beef jerky and coffee, since we'll have to camp there until dusk."

"You really were making arrangements this morning, weren't you?"

"Of course. What did you think I might be doing?"

She shrugged and looked uncomfortable. "I thought perhaps you might be talking to the *federales*."

"Why would I do that, Victoria?"

She shrugged again, looking embarrassed.

"I'm sorry," she said. "I trust you; I really do."

It was his turn to look uncomfortable. "We'd better get going," he said.

Jalapa was a tiny little town of several adobe build-

ings and a few wooden frame ones. Victoria told Clint
that it did not have a hotel or a sheriff, but that it did
have a cantina with a couple of girls working in the
back.

"It's just a rest stop, then," he concluded.

"A rest stop?"

"Yes, a place where outlaws—or bandits—can come
to rest without fear of being caught by the law."

"That's true," she said. "That is why Benito picked
the beach near here for the exchange."

"How will he be getting the payment here?" he
asked as they rode through Jalapa.

"He will have to use a buckboard," she said.

"That much cash?"

"There are many pieces of silver and gold that he
. . . found," she said. He was sure that she had been
going to say, that he stole, and caught herself.

"Heavy pieces?"

"Yes."

"How long will it take him to get here?"

"Not long."

That meant that Benito must have hidden the stuff
nearby. Could he have hidden it somewhere in Jalapa
itself? He didn't think so. The town was too small to
allow for that.

As they passed the cantina, Clint said, "Should we
stop for a drink?"

Victoria looked around nervously—still looking for
federales—and said, "Why not?"

There were four other horses tied off in front of the
cantina, so business seemed to be booming for the tiny
town of Jalapa. They secured their animals and then
went inside.

As he stepped through the door, Clint suddenly knew

something was wrong. He could feel it even before he saw the men at the bar.

"Uh-uh," he said, putting a hand out to stop Victoria and quickly move her to his left side, away from his gun hand.

"What is it?"

He didn't answer. He saw one of the men turning away from the bar and knew that it was too late to back out without being seen.

The man was Sanchez, the brother of the sheriff in Nuevo Laredo.

Immediately, recognition came into the man's eyes and he went for his gun, shouting to his friends.

Clint reacted instantly, pushing Victoria away with his left hand and drawing his own gun with his right. He fired before Sanchez was able to reach his gun, his bullet striking the man in the chest, but by then the others had turned and were reaching for their guns.

The Gunsmith fell into a crouch and fired a second time, catching one man in the forehead. He killed a third man with no problem, but as he moved to his left, Victoria moved to her right and bumped into him, throwing him slightly off balance.

"Oh," she said as he grabbed her and shoved her away again. He turned his attention to a fourth man and saw too late that he was going to fire.

White-hot pain seared his left shoulder as he fired desperately. His bullet caught the last man before he could fire again, and the man slid to the floor to join his three dead friends.

Clint rose, staggered, and groped for a table to lean on. He missed and fell onto his right side, holding onto his gun.

"Clint!" Victoria cried, rushing to his side. The bartender, who had dropped down behind the bar when the shooting started, stood up now and stared in awe at the gringo who had outdrawn and killed four Mexicans.

Instinctively he knew that the wound was not that bad. He could still move the arm, and as Victoria reached him he was in the act of standing up. She put her arm around his waist to assist him.

"Are you all right?"

"Yes," he said, examining his shoulder. "The bullet went through. Get some whiskey and something to use as a bandage."

"You need a doctor."

"Is there one in Jalapa?" he asked.

"I don't know," she answered. "I will ask—"

"There's not enough time. Do what I say. We'll have to take care of it ourselves."

He holstered his gun, pulled a chair over, and sat down while she went to get him the things he asked for. While he was waiting, he pulled his shirt down off his shoulder so he could take a closer look at the wound. It was bleeding freely, but he could still move the arm which meant nothing vital had been torn. It hurt like hell, but that was about it. If they could stop the bleeding, he would be all right until they could reach a doctor.

When she returned with the whiskey and some dubious looking strips of cloth for bandages, he grabbed the whiskey and took a healthy swallow that took his breath away.

"All right," he said hoarsely, handing the bottle back to her, "pour it on both sides of the wound, and then make a bandage—and make it tight."

She did as he asked and when the whiskey touched his injured flesh he sucked air through his teeth, but did not cry out. She handed him the bottle so she could tie the bandage, and he took another swallow.

"All right?" she asked.

"Yeah," he said, "it's nice and tight."

"What will we do now?"

"Give me a few minutes," he said, suddenly feeling dizzy, "and then we'll get going."

"Clint, you're so pale."

He was pale, and he was sweating, but he knew that was from the shock of the blow. As long as the wound didn't get infected, he would be all right until he could see a doctor.

At least, that's what he hoped.

It was a half hour before Clint was able to get to his feet and walk out to his horse.

"Can you get on?" Victoria asked.

"Just get up on your horse and don't worry," he said.

As she walked around to her horse, he grabbed the saddle horn and hoisted himself up into the saddle. He experienced a moment of vertigo, closed his eyes, and waited it out.

"Are you all right?" Victoria asked.

"I'm fine," he said. "Let's ride."

THIRTY

"We're here," Victoria said in a low voice.

It was almost as if she were afraid to wake him up, and in fact he *had* dozed off in the saddle. Cowboys often dozed in the saddle, secure enough in their seat to know that they wouldn't fall out, especially if they had a good mount.

In Duke, Clint Adams had the best.

He opened his eyes and looked around. Duke's hooves were in sand and the Gulf of Mexico loomed ahead of him. The breeze coming off the water felt good and he actually felt revived.

"How are you?"

"Pretty good," he said. He moved his left arm experimentally. There was some soreness, but beyond that it seemed operational.

He was just glad it hadn't been his right shoulder that had been injured. Although he was able to handle a gun well with his left hand, it did not match the skill of his right.

"Let's move over there," he suggested, indicating a

173

large sand dune. "We can put the horses behind it where they won't be seen."

"Who are we hiding from?"

"I don't know," he said, "I'd just feel safer if we saw whoever was coming before they saw us."

It wasn't much farther, Benito realized with elation. Soon he'd be at the beach, waiting for the ship that was carrying the weapons that were the future of the revolution. Already he could smell the salt in the air from the ocean.

Tired, but smiling broadly, he tried to coax more speed out of his tired horse, uncaring as to whether or not he pushed it to death.

The revolution came first.

James Butler was feeling pretty pleased with himself. He, Chico, Delores, and the other five men had managed to leave the camp early without waking the other men. Luckily, the watch was given to one of the men who had come over to his side.

He knew that Delores had been taking them in circles and it amused him. He knew that the exchange would probably be set for just before nightfall, so that both sides could move out afterwards under the cover of darkness, so at midday he pulled to a halt and looked over at Benito's wife.

Her face was bruised, her lips swollen, and the ache in her lower abdomen and buttocks made it difficult to sit on her horse. After he had managed to persuade her to take them to the site of the exchange, he had forced himself on her.

"Delores," he said, and she looked at him listlessly.

"This is as far as you go."

"What?"

He pulled one of his guns from his sash and pointed it at her.

"If you kill me," she said, panicking, "you will never get what you want."

"I'm not gonna get it anyway, woman," he said. "You been taking us in circles, and I'm getting dizzy, so this is where you get off."

He cocked the hammer on his gun and she cried out, "Wait!"

"Why?"

"I will take you to the place," she said, "the beach near Jalapa."

He could have killed her then, but he knew how long the beach was and they might find the spot too late.

"All right," he said, easing the hammer back down and tucking the gun into his sash. "Show the way—but remember this is your last chance."

"I will remember."

"Someone is coming," Victoria said.

Clint's head jerked up and his eyes opened. Damn, he'd been nodding off again.

"Where?"

"Listen?"

He listened and heard it, the clatter of an approaching buckboard that sounded as if it had seen better days. It was creaking and whining beneath a heavy load.

He got to his feet with some difficulty, weathered another bout of vertigo, and walked out from behind the sand dune. He did not see that Victoria had been prepared to catch him if he stumbled or fell.

"That is Benito," she said.

"About time," he said under his breath. His shoulder felt sore and there was a burning sensation around the wound."

"And here come the guns," he heard her say.

He turned and stared out into the water and saw the ship. It was still some distance off, but he could see her white sails clearly.

"All we need now is the rest of the ban—rebels."

"They will be along."

That was what he was afraid of. It occurred to him that by this time the man he was looking for might have been accepted by the bandits as one of them. They might not take kindly to his being badmouthed—or worse—by the Gunsmith.

They watched and waited while Benito drew closer with the buckboard. He pulled it to a stop before the wheels hit the sand, and he dropped down from the seat.

His first question might have been expected.

"Where is Manuel?"

It was Victoria who answered before Clint had a chance to open his mouth.

"He's dead, Benito."

"Dead?" he asked. He was dusty and dirty and his eyes stood out against the dusty pallor of his skin. "My brother is dead?"

"Yes. I'm sorry."

"How did it happen?" he demanded, and then looking at Clint he asked, "Who killed him?"

"We don't know," she said. "The soldiers found him and I didn't think it wise to ask them about it."

"I will ask them," he said, looking back at her.

"After the revolution," she said.

Benito opened his mouth to make a sharp reply, then thought better of it, and nodded, saying, "After the revolution."

Clint walked over to the buckboard to examine the booty that Benito was using to finance his revolution.

"Do not touch that!" Benito said sharply.

"Just curious," Clint said. He grasped the edge of the tarp that was covering everything and pulled it back. The flat bed of the buckboard was littered with everything from silverware to what looked like gold teeth. There was a chest that he felt sure was holding whatever cash there was.

"Looks like an odd assortment of items, Benito," he said. He picked up the candle holder and said, "Where did this come from?"

"That is none of your business."

"Looks to me like it might have come off the altar of a church."

"It was donated to the cause," Benito said.

"I'm sure," Clint replied, dropping it back onto the buckboard.

Benito looked at his shoulder and said, "You are wounded. Are you sure you do not know how my brother died?"

"Clint was wounded in Jalapa," Victoria said. "Four men tried to kill him, but he killed them instead."

"Old friends?" Benito asked.

"Old enemies," Clint said. "We've got a bottle of whiskey that I've been using to sorta kill the pain. You're welcome to some of it."

Benito hesitated, then said, "*Gracias*. I *am* thirsty."

Victoria fetched the bottle and handed it to Benito. He took a long drink, then handed it to Clint, who finished it.

"Look," Victoria called out.

They both turned to see what had caught her attention and saw that the ship had stopped. It had covered the distance faster than Clint had thought possible, but then he didn't know much about boats.

"They're dropping a smaller boat into the water," he noticed. "Guess they're getting ready to make their delivery."

"Then I guess we'd better make our withdrawal and move on," another voice said from behind them.

They turned and saw a man standing at the top of the sand dune, holding a gun on them. Five men came out from the other side, one of them pushing a battered woman ahead of them. Clint Adams, however, only had eyes for the man on the dune. He was wearing a red sash around his waist and had a pair of twin .32s in his hand.

His heart began to pound as he stared at the ghost of Wild Bill Hickok.

THIRTY-ONE

After studying the man, Clint had to admit it was uncanny. He *looked* a lot like Wild Bill Hickok.

But he wasn't.

He looked like him; he wore the red sash and carried the twin .32s that Bill favored, but he wasn't Hickok.

"You're not Bill Hickok."

The man looked at Clint and said, "Who are you?"

"Name's Clint Adams."

"The Gunsmith?"

"That's right."

"You and Hickok were friends."

"Right again."

"Well, to tell you the truth, Gunsmith, I never actually claimed to be Hickok. Folks just seemed to make that assumption because of the way I like to dress."

"You dressed that way so people *would* think you were Hickok," Clint accused.

"Ah, maybe so," the man said. "That doesn't matter now. Chico, check the buckboard."

"Chico, what is this?" Benito demanded. "How could you steal from the revolution?"

''Go ahead, Chico,'' the man said. ''There is no revolution, Benito. It's all been in your head. Your men
are lucky I'm doing this because now they'll get to live
a little longer.''

''The revolution will go on—''

''Sure, friend,'' the man with the red sash said, ''you
go ahead and take the President's Palace—but you'll
have to do it without those guns.''

''It is all here, but it is heavy,'' Chico shouted. He
had opened the chest and was holding money in both
hands. Clint wondered how many people Benito had to
steal from to get that much money.

''We'll take the buckboard.''

''What if they follow?''

''They won't,'' the man said.

''What name do you go by?'' Clint asked.

The man looked at him and said, ''I've been using
Butler, James Butler. Clever, huh?''

''Very. What's your real name?''

''That don't matter,'' he said. ''When I leave here,
I'll be so rich I'll probably go through a dozen names.''

''You're not leaving here,'' Clint said.

''What makes you say that?''

''My men will be here soon,'' Benito said.

''Your men are hours behind us,'' Butler said. ''Oh,
by the way, thanks for the use of your wife, but I'm
through with her now.''

One of the men pushed Delores and she stumbled toward her husband. As she reached him, Benito grabbed
her, used her as a shield, and went for his gun.

Clint had to admit that the man who called himself
Butler was good. He fired and hit Benito right in the
face, the only part of the man that was clear of the
woman.

The Gunsmith drew and killed the man who had pushed the woman first. The others were slow to react, and Clint had a chance to fire at Butler. It felt funny shooting at a man who looked that much like Hickok— so funny in fact that he actually hesitated. That moment's hesitation cost him as Butler dropped off the sand dune, seeking cover behind it.

Clint couldn't afford to hesitate again. Butler's other men were grabbing for their guns. He fired and downed another one and heard a shot from his right. A third man fell and Clint had his choice of the remaining two men. He dropped to one knee to present a smaller target, and the movement caused pain to flare through his shoulder.

Chico had dropped his fists of money and was clawing for his gun when Clint shot him in the stomach. He heard an exchange of shots to his right, and when he looked, he saw that Victoria had grabbed Benito's gun and killed two of the bandits for him—but had taken a bullet herself.

"Clint," she said, blood gushing from a hole in her chest.

On the ground near her, Benito was dead, and his wife was lying atop him with a hole in her back.

Victoria fell but Clint couldn't go to her. He flattened himself against the front of the sand dune because James Butler was still alive.

He began to inch his way around the dune. Butler and his men must have left their horses a distance away in order to sneak up to them on foot. Butler was either on the other side of the dune or he was on the run toward his horse. Clint opted for the former because he didn't think the man would leave without the money and booty on the buckboard.

Clint continued to inch around the sand dune until he was almost to the other side. He looked behind him to see if Butler hadn't worked his way all the way around behind him, and then he looked up.

He'd made a mistake. Butler had jumped down off the dune, waited until the shooting was over, and then climbed back up. He was standing there now, pointing his guns at Clint with a smile on his face.

"Let's see how fast you are now, Gunsmith," he said, and Clint knew he'd never get his gun up in time.

From far away he heard a shot and something punched into Butler's chest. The smile faded from his face and was replaced—first by a puzzled look, and then by one of horror. He toppled forward and fell at the Gunsmith's feet, dead.

Upon closer inspection, he didn't look all that much like Bill, after all.

THIRTY-TWO

"And what happened to Benito's men?" Jonathan Braxton asked.

They were in Braxton's den, enjoying brandy after dinner, and Carlotta was sitting nearby, listening intently. She had tears in her eyes from Clint's description of how Victoria had died, essentially saving Clint's life.

"They came riding along at that point," Clint said, "but so did the *federales* and other soldiers. You see, that morning I made a deal with Lieutenant Valdez to have his men lay back until I got what I wanted, and then they could come in to get what they wanted."

"So the two forces nearly ran into each other," Braxton said.

"And Valdez and his men—and the *federales*—ran them down. I'm very grateful to Paco, by the way. He made a fine shot from that small boat."

"He saw that you were in trouble, and he also saw the *federales*. After he made that shot, he simply turned the boat around and went back to the ship. His quick thinking not only saved your life; it saved me some embarrassment. I think I will give him a raise.''

"He deserves it,'' Clint said.

"I'm sorry about Miss Victoria. You mustn't feel that you betrayed her. You saved the lives of many people because that revolution was destined to fail.''

"I know,'' Clint said. That had worried him when he was making the deal with Valdez, but his real aim had been to save Victoria's life, and she had died, anyway.

"What about my offer?''

"The partnership?'' Clint asked. "Now that the revolution is over?''

"There will be other revolutions,'' Braxton said, "in other places. And there is always a market for guns. What do you say?''

"I'm sorry, Jonathan,'' Clint said. "I think I'll just keep moving on.''

"Well, you are welcome here any time, my friend, and the offer is always open. More brandy?'' Clint declined the additional brandy.

As Braxton poured himself more brandy, he saw that Carlotta was watching him, and Clint was looking forward to the time when Braxton would retire for the night because he was eagerly anticipating losing himself for a while in Carlotta's sweetness and warmth.

"I'm sorry you didn't find your friend alive,'' Braxton said then.

"I'm not.''

"Why?''

"If I had,'' Clint said, swirling the remaining liquid in his glass, "I would have given him holy hell, and I don't think Wild Bill Hickok and I ever had a real fight in all the time we knew each other. After he was dead would have been a hell of a time to start.''

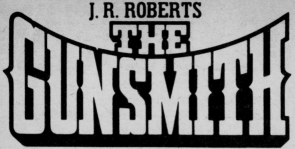

J. R. ROBERTS
THE GUNSMITH

SERIES

☐ 30896-1	THE GUNSMITH #25: NORTH OF THE BORDER	$2.50
☐ 30897-X	THE GUNSMITH #26: EAGLE'S GAP	$2.50
☐ 30900-3	THE GUNSMITH #28: THE PANHANDLE SEARCH	$2.50
☐ 30902-X	THE GUNSMITH #29: WILDCAT ROUND-UP	$2.50
☐ 30903-8	THE GUNSMITH #30: THE PONDEROSA WAR	$2.50
☐ 30904-6	THE GUNSMITH #31: TROUBLE RIDES A FAST HORSE	$2.50
☐ 30911-9	THE GUNSMITH #32: DYNAMITE JUSTICE	$2.50
☐ 30912-7	THE GUNSMITH #33: THE POSSE	$2.50
☐ 30913-5	THE GUNSMITH #34: NIGHT OF THE GILA	$2.50
☐ 30914-3	THE GUNSMITH #35: THE BOUNTY WOMEN	$2.50
☐ 30915-1	THE GUNSMITH #36: BLACK PEARL SALOON	$2.50
☐ 30935-6	THE GUNSMITH #37: GUNDOWN IN PARADISE	$2.50
☐ 30936-4	THE GUNSMITH #38: KING OF THE BORDER	$2.50
☐ 30940-2	THE GUNSMITH #39: THE EL PASO SALT WAR	$2.50
☐ 30941-0	THE GUNSMITH #40: THE TEN PINES KILLER	$2.50
☐ 30942-9	THE GUNSMITH #41: HELL WITH A PISTOL	$2.50
☐ 30946-1	THE GUNSMITH #42: THE WYOMING CATTLE KILL	$2.50
☐ 30947-X	THE GUNSMITH #43: THE GOLDEN HORSEMAN	$2.50
☐ 30948-8	THE GUNSMITH #44: THE SCARLET GUN	$2.50
☐ 30949-6	THE GUNSMITH #45: NAVAHO DEVIL	$2.50
☐ 30950-X	THE GUNSMITH #46: WILD BILL'S GHOST	$2.50

Prices may be slightly higher in Canada.

JAKE LOGAN

Prices may be slightly higher in Canada.